"It might be interesting to get to know each other again."

Esme continued to stare at him. "I can't think what else there is to know," she responded at length. "You're Jack Doyle, Internet entrepreneur and new owner of Highfield. I'm Esme Hamilton, single mother of one and ex-cleaner of your mansion. Do you think we have any common ground?"

"Is it Highfield?" he asked bluntly. "Is that the problem? You can't bear for me, the cook's son, to have it?"

Esme's eyes widened at the slant he'd put on things. The animosity she felt was unconnected to house deeds and family origins.

"A little tip for the future, though. If you really don't like a man, it's best not to make those little moaning sounds when he's kissing you. Might give him the whole wrong idea."

Alison Fraser

THE MOTHER AND THE MILLIONAIRE

MISTRESS
TO A
MILLIONAIRE

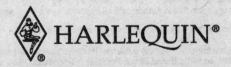

HARLEQUIN®

TORONTO • NEW YORK • LONDON
AMSTERDAM • PARIS • SYDNEY • HAMBURG
STOCKHOLM • ATHENS • TOKYO • MILAN • MADRID
PRAGUE • WARSAW • BUDAPEST • AUCKLAND

ISBN 0-373-12251-9

THE MOTHER AND THE MILLIONAIRE

First North American Publication 2002.

Copyright © 2001 by Alison Fraser.

Visit us at www.eHarlequin.com

Printed in U.S.A.

CHAPTER ONE

IT WAS one of those life-changing moments. For Esme, any-way. She opened the door and there he was. Not so different. Older, of course. Better-dressed, too, in dark suit and silk tie. But essentially the same.

'*Midge?*' He half smiled, uncertain whether it was her.

She didn't smile back. She was sick with shock. It was as if he'd just risen from the dead.

'Jack Doyle.' He identified himself.

Quite unnecessary. A towering six feet two, dark-haired and grey-eyed, with razor-sharp cheekbones and a wicked smile, he wasn't easy to forget.

She struggled to collect her thoughts, only to find herself stammering. 'I—I—I...'

All her hard-won composure out of the window. A de-cade's worth. Back to the gawky teenager, cursed with puppy fat and the awful nickname Midge.

Speech proved impossible. Just as well or she might have said, *Go away. I have a life now.*

And he wouldn't have understood.

He took advantage of her silence to do an inventory. Heavy-lidded grey eyes travelled from her coiled blonde hair and fine-boned face to her slim figure in an A-line dress, and back again.

'Who would have thought it—little Midge all grown up?' His voice was teasing rather than mocking.

Midge knew that—no, Esme; that was her name—knew that, but it didn't help. Still, it rescued her from incoherence.

'No one calls me that now.' She finally spoke and, looking down her nose, added, 'May I help you?'

Polite veneer barely masking condescension.

He got it, of course. She'd expected him to. Doyle had

5

always been quick on the uptake. Brilliantly so apart from when it concerned her sister, Arabella.

'Scary,' he commented.

'What?' she demanded, unable to help herself.

He shook his head but a smile played on his mouth. He was laughing at something.

She remembered that of old, too. Jack Doyle watching her family as if they were interesting curiosities, unable to comment because of their respective positions, but commenting all the same with the curve of his lips or the lift of a brow.

'You haven't changed!' she accused.

'You have,' he accused in return. 'Very lady of the manor.'

Esme glowered but was unable to argue, considering she had just borrowed her mother's airs and graces to try and put him down. Unsuccessfully.

'Better than being mannerless,' she threw back at length.

He looked surprised, as well he might. He might have been the cook's son, educated at the local county school, but Jack Doyle had always known how to behave.

His eyes narrowed slightly before he responded, 'Well, you'll know how that feels soon. Being man*or*less yourselves, I mean.'

So he'd heard. The manor was to be sold.

'Is that supposed to be a joke?'

'No.'

She hadn't thought so. More a cruel remark. That surprised *her*. She didn't remember that side of him.

'Is your mother about?' he added. 'Her *lady*ship, should I say?'

'No, actually you shouldn't,' she corrected. 'My mother remarried.'

'Of course,' he concluded, 'and presumably lost the title. Poor old Rosie. That must have been traumatic for her.'

It had been. In fact, her mother, Rosalind—who had never allowed anyone to call her Rosie in her life—had been very slow to take a second walk up the aisle. Only an ultimatum from her new husband had forced the issue.

'Is she around?' he asked.

'No.'

'Arabella?' he added casually.

But Esme wasn't fooled. Jack Doyle had never been casual where Arabella was concerned.

'No, she's in New York,' Esme relayed, then, after a pause, 'With her husband.'

She watched for a reaction but there was none. Jack had always kept his emotions under wraps. Well, almost always.

'She lives there?' was all he said.

'At the moment,' she confirmed.

It wasn't a lie. Arabella would be there for some time yet. Just as being with her husband wasn't a lie. No need to tell this man that the two were sitting on opposite sides of a divorce court.

'Well, I'd really love to chat—' she curled her hand round the doorknob '—but I'm expecting someone.'

'Yes, I know.' The amused look was back on his face.

It was a moment or so before Esme caught on. 'You're it—the man from Jadenet?'

He gave a nod. 'I'm it—or *he,* to be more precise.'

Jack watched her changing expression, but found he couldn't interpret it. Initially he'd been pleased when Esme had been the one to appear at the door. He had always liked her. The best of the Scott-Hamiltons. Now she was so much prettier—beautiful, even—but had also grown disappointingly similar to her mother.

'Phone the estate agent,' he suggested, 'check my credentials if you like.'

He proffered her his mobile phone.

Esme ignored it, her uncertain look turning into a positive scowl. She believed him but his whole attitude riled her.

'You have no idea, have you?' she accused.

Doyle frowned. He imagined he'd been trying to help her. 'Obviously not.'

'Do you know how many years there's been Scott-Hamiltons in this house?' she demanded with atypical arrogance.

'Don't tell me,' he drawled back, 'since the Magna Carta?'

Having never been a great history student, Esme hadn't the first idea when that was, but it was scarcely relevant, as he was laughing at her.

He always had, only in the past there had been a degree of fondness in it.

'What's the point?' she dismissed at length. 'You wouldn't understand.'

'Being of simple peasant stock, you mean?' he concluded, an edge behind the banter now.

Esme was left wishing she hadn't started this. She was coming over as the snob of the century, and that wasn't really her at all. Jack Doyle had just thrown her off balance.

'I didn't say that.'

'You didn't have to. I know what your family thought of me. I heard it from the horse's mouth, remember?'

Esme coloured. She remembered. She was unlikely to forget, having her own memento from that day.

'I always thought you were different, though, Midge.' Dark grey eyes studied her once more.

Esme wanted to say, I was different. I *am* different. But it seemed so much safer to hide behind the class barrier.

'Don't call me Midge,' was all she eventually muttered. 'I'm not ten any more.'

'No.' Jack underlined the word as he noted once again the new Esme. Slim and long-legged but shapely where it counted, at breasts and hips. 'I can see that.'

His eyes stopped just short of undressing her. One of life's ironies. Ten years ago she had longed for him to look at her this way. Now it was anathema to her.

'Papers,' she almost barked at him, 'I assume you have some.'

'Papers?'

'To prove you have a viewing appointment.'

Jack's mouth tightened as he wondered who Miss High and Mighty Scott-Hamilton thought she was—or who he was, for that matter.

He reached a hand into the inside pocket of his suit and took out his wallet. From it he withdrew a business card.

It was extended with a thin-lipped smile and Esme didn't need clairvoyance to know she'd annoyed him. She took the card but, without her reading glasses, the small print danced in front of her. Perhaps it would have with her glasses on, thrown back as she had been to her past.

She screwed up her eyes and the print started to come into focus, but not before he suggested, 'I'll read it for you if you like.'

This time his tone was milder, less sarcastic, but it still sliced through her. Midge wasn't the only nickname bestowed on her by her big sister Arabella when they were children, only she'd confined the use of Dumbo to outside parental range.

'I'm not that thick, you know!' she snapped back.

He looked surprised, as if such a thought had never crossed his mind. 'Have I ever suggested you were, Mi—Esme?'

In fairness, no. He was the one who'd suggested otherwise.

'I just remember you wearing reading glasses,' he added.

She cringed a little. Was she forever printed on his mind as a plump, bespectacled teen? At the time she'd longed for him to look her way, to notice. It seemed he had. She just hadn't measured up.

She stared back down at the card until the bold lettering came into focus:

Jack Doyle
Managing Director
J.D. Net

She didn't bother scrutinising the telephone number. She was too busy absorbing the rest. He was MD and it wasn't Jadenet as she'd heard her mother say—but J.D. Net. As in, Jack Doyle Net?

What else had her mother said about their prospective buyer? Some American internet entrepreneur worth megabucks. Had her mother been in the dark or was she too proud to admit the truth?

'Does my mother know J.D. Net is you?' she asked bluntly.

He shrugged. 'Possibly not. I didn't arrange this viewing in person.'

No, he would have lackeys to do that. Go buy my child-hood home, he'd probably said. Only technically it wasn't. The cottage in the grounds where he'd lived was the one thing held back in the sale. She assumed he knew that.

'You'd better come in,' she said finally, and left him to follow her into the hall.

It was stark and bare. What furniture her mother hadn't wanted had been auctioned off. She had tried to auction the house, too, but it hadn't made its reserve price and now they were struggling to find a buyer.

The chequered marble on the floor was worn but still mag-nificent. Jack Doyle looked up towards the sweeping staircase and the galleried landing above.

Esme watched him assessing, measuring, perhaps trying to picture it with his own taste of decor and furniture.

Eventually he walked towards the drawing room, his foot-steps echoing in the hall, and opened the double doors to glance inside. He seemed to be taking brief mental snapshots, repeating the process for each of the main rooms until he reached what had been the dining room.

There he lingered. The room was bare but Esme wondered if he remembered how it was the night he'd barged in, look-ing for Arabella. Esme had sat at the window end of the long table, Rosalind Scott-Hamilton at the other. No Arabella. She'd left their mother to act as go-between, a task the older woman had seemed to relish. Esme had burned with humil-iation on his behalf.

She was brought back sharply to the present as he finally turned to face her, his expression neutral. 'I'd like to look round upstairs.'

Esme shrugged her permission. She knew she should be trying to sell the house and its good points but she couldn't bring herself to do it—not to him, anyway.

Jack started to climb the stairs and she followed automatically. When he paused at the landing window where the stairs forked into two, Esme ventured, 'Was it always an ambition—to come back and buy this place?'

Of course, it was a silly thing to ask. He was hardly likely to confess such cupidity.

His lips twisted slightly. 'I see your reading taste hasn't altered.'

Esme looked blank at this *non sequitur.* 'I don't know what you mean.'

'Jane Eyre?' He raised a quizzical brow. 'Or was it *Wuthering Heights?* The one where the uncouth stable boy returns a rich man to wreak havoc on the family.'

'Wuthering Heights,' she responded, although she suspected he knew the answer.

He nodded to the view outside, stone terraces and cultivated lawns leading down to disused tennis courts, the maze and a small lake beyond. 'Not exactly Heathcliff territory, is it? Don't think I'll hear Cathy calling for me out there.'

He was laughing at her. What else?

Esme knew how to wipe the smile from his face and did so, saying, 'Don't you mean Arabella?'

'Arabella?' His mouth thinned slightly. 'As the Great Love of my life, you mean?'

She hadn't expected him to be so upfront about it. Nor had she expected it to still hurt—his preference for her big sister. But it did.

Then he added, 'Well, sorry to disappoint but I've moved on from there. I've had at least two or three Great Loves since then,' he informed her, very much tongue-in-cheek.

Esme answered in kind, 'How wonderful for you—and them, of course,' hiding her real feelings behind sarcasm.

What else could she do? Tell him what a pig of a time she'd been having while he was living the life of Reilly? It wouldn't be true, anyway. She and Harry were happy enough.

Jack was taken aback for a moment—this new Esme really had grown claws—but found himself amused despite the fact.

'I'll take that as a vote of confidence,' he said as she began leading the way to the first-floor gallery.

'I wouldn't,' Esme muttered under her breath but loud enough for him to hear.

Jack chose to ignore the comment but, wanting to set the record straight, continued, 'Anyway, it's more a coincidence, us buying this place.'

Us? Esme picked that up and pondered over it. Us as in his business, or us as in significant other?

'We need a base near London. Sussex is well-placed for the Continent and Highfield is one of three possibilities the location agency came up with,' he relayed as she showed him the first of the twelve upstairs rooms. 'Unfortunately our first choice was sold off before we were in a position to move on it and the other place has no permission for business use, so that leaves Highfield.'

He made it sound as if he might *settle* for the house. Her beloved home. One of the finest Georgian manors in the area.

'Never mind,' she rallied, striding in and out of bedrooms like a demented estate agent, 'it has at least one point in its favour.'

'Which is?' Jack followed in her wake and, leaning against a door jamb, forced her to come to rest.

'Well, you could always claim it's your family seat,' Esme volunteered recklessly, resentfully. 'Impress your other *nouveau riche* friends.'

She knew she'd gone too far even before she said it. She just didn't care.

She wanted to pierce that seamless confidence. Hurt him as he'd hurt her, however unknowingly. Because suddenly it seemed worse that he *didn't* know, had never known, hadn't the first idea of the tears she'd cried for him, the pain she'd endured.

For a moment Jack didn't react at all. The truth was he wasn't sure how to. It was as if the family terrier, cute and loveable, had suddenly turned into a teeth-baring Rottweiler, guarding her territory.

Only it wasn't hers for much longer, whether he bought it or someone else did. He'd gathered that much from the location agent. And, yes, though it held some appeal—the idea

that Rosalind Scott-Hamilton would eventually discover it was the cook's son who had bought her stately pile—it wasn't part of some grand master plan. He would pass on it if it proved unsuitable.

'You may have something there,' he replied in dry tones. 'Crest of arms on the door and my portrait above the mantelpiece—what do you think?'

Esme *thought* he was laughing at her again.

'I'll give you the commission if you like,' he added.

'Me?'

'You were something of an artist, as I recall.'

'That was in the past.'

'But you went to art college?'

That had been Esme's intention but reality had intruded.

'No, I did other things,' she dismissed.

Jack waited for her to expand on that statement but she remained tight-lipped. He guessed she'd probably gone down the finishing school-debutante route that her sister her taken. Was that what had changed her?

'Do you want to see the other rooms?' she asked offhandedly.

It drew the response, 'Do you want to sell the house?'

She flushed. Did she want to sell the house? No. Did they have to? Yes.

'I'm sorry.' Somehow she gritted out the words. 'I wasn't sure if you were still interested.'

'Well, I won't be if I don't see it all,' he pointed out.

'Right.' Teeth clenched, Esme continued the guided tour.

At each room, she became increasingly conscious of how bare and decaying the whole house looked. Only her old sanctuary still had furniture. A bed, washstand, bookcase and chest of drawers were earmarked for her new home but she had been slow in arranging for the pieces to be moved.

'Your room?' Jack guessed, seeing the book titles on a shelf.

She nodded.

'Are you still living here?' he added, frowning a little.

'No,' she replied shortly. 'Everything will be gone by the time the house is sold on.'

'Where are you based now?' It was a natural enough question.

She gave a deliberately vague, 'Locally.'

'Are you married?' he added with mild curiosity.

The question made her inexplicably cross. 'Who would I be married to?'

She recognised the oddity of her answer, even before he gave her a quizzical look.

'Well, there was that boy,' he replied with a slight smile, 'from one of the neighbouring estates. You used to go riding with him. Sandy-haired. One of a few brothers?'

Esme knew who he meant but didn't help him out. There had been no real romance with Henry Fairfax.

Instead she said, 'Jack, you've been away almost ten years. Do you imagine everyone else's life has stood still?'

'Fair comment.' He pulled an apologetic face. 'But people do get frozen in time if you haven't seen them for a while.'

Esme supposed he was right. Up until today—until just this hour—Jack Doyle had stayed in her head as her first love, a love tainted by anguish for a young man she'd idolised.

Now here he was, far too real, and bringing with him feelings of resentment that had somehow never properly surfaced till now.

'So what is it that the new Esme does?' he enquired with a smile.

The interest could have been genuine but Esme didn't think so. Had he ever really noticed her with Arabella around?

'I *do* people's houses,' she replied shortly.

'Do?' he echoed. 'As in…what exactly?'

He sounded hesitant, unusual for him.

Esme glanced at him briefly. Something in his expression helped her read his mind. God, he really did think the family had fallen on hard times!

She was almost amused. Certainly amused enough to play along. 'How do people normally *do* houses?'

'You *clean* them?' he said with lingering incredulity.

No, she actually decorated them, but she was enjoying his confusion too much to say so.

'Have you a problem with that?' she rejoined.

'No, of course not.' His own mother, though officially cook, had cleaned up after the Scott-Hamiltons. 'It just isn't something I pictured you doing.'

'Well, that's life,' Esme concluded philosophically. 'I never pictured you a big-shot wheeler-dealer businessman.'

'Hardly that,' he denied. 'I design and market websites. That just happens to be where the money is now.'

It wasn't false modesty. Esme knew that much. Even as a young man, Jack Doyle had never underplayed or overstated his achievements. He'd sailed through school and college, a straight 'A' student, but, being totally secure about his intellectual gifts, had felt no need to advertise them.

It was Esme's father who had noticed and come up with the idea of him tutoring Esme. Up till then the cook's son had done work in the stables or on the home farm or thinning out the wood. But, with his brains, surely he would be better employed doing something about Esme?

Looking back it was a mad idea. Why should a seventeen-year-old boy, however clever, manage to help eleven-year-old Esme when her expensive prep school had failed miserably?

But he had. That was the even crazier thing. He'd been the one to notice Esme could remember perfectly anything she was taught verbally, could talk with intelligence on most subjects and only descended into gibberish when committing to paper. Remarkably, he'd been the first to suggest dyslexia as a possibility, and tests had proved him right.

Esme found herself treading down memory lane once more and pulled herself back sharply.

'And money is important?' she remarked for something to say.

'It is if you haven't got any,' he responded quite equably.

Esme didn't argue. She knew he was talking from experience. His mother had died from cancer just after his finals, keeping her illness secret almost to the end. Accompanied by Jack, she had gone home to her native Ireland for a holiday and passed away there. She had left nothing but the money for her funeral. If Jack had grieved, he'd done it alone.

She watched him now, gazing through her bedroom window. It faced the back of the house and offered a view of the stable block and woods beyond. In autumn, when the trees were bare, it was just possible to see the chimney of the gamekeeper's cottage where Jack had lived with his mother. But it was currently spring and greenery obscured it.

It was in his mind, however, as he said, 'I understand the cottage is rented out.'

Esme's stomach tightened a little but she kept her cool. 'Yes, it is. You know it's not part of the sale?'

He turned. 'No, I didn't. There's no mention in the particulars.'

Esme glanced towards the folder in his hand. She'd not perused the estate agent's details. She'd trusted her mother's word instead.

'I don't really see how it could be excluded,' he continued, 'considering it's in the middle of the estate.'

'Well, it is!' Esme snapped with a certainty she was far from feeling.

Jack shrugged, unwilling to argue, commenting instead, 'Perhaps that's why you're having difficulty selling—people buy these estates for privacy.'

Esme wondered if he was going out of his way to upset. 'Who says we're having difficulty selling?'

'The fact,' he replied, 'that the estate has been on the market over a year, perhaps... Is it a sitting tenant, the person in the cottage?'

'Why?' Esme had no idea what *she* was.

'Just that if you're worried about getting them to vacate,' he relayed, 'there are ways and means.'

'Ways and means?' Esme's eyes rounded. 'What exactly do you mean?'

'Well, we could send a couple of heavies to persuade him to move on.' Jack read her mind with uncanny accuracy. 'Or, alternatively, we could offer him a generous sum to help with relocation. Personally, I prefer the latter method. Slightly more civilised,' he finished, tongue very firmly in cheek.

He'd wrongfooted her again and Esme felt herself regressing further and further to the girl called Midge whom he'd teased so sweetly she'd ended up adoring him.

Only it didn't feel sweet any more, just patronising, maybe even a little cruel.

'The cottage isn't for sale.' She repeated what she'd first stated.

He was unimpressed. 'Let's see what your mother says, assuming I'm interested.'

'You're going to talk to my mother?' She didn't conceal her surprise.

He raised a brow in return. 'Is there any reason I shouldn't?'

Was he kidding? Esme could think of at least one but didn't want to voice it aloud.

His eyes narrowed, scrutinising her expression. 'Unless you think it inadvisable?'

'Well—' she pulled a face '—you didn't...um...part on the best of terms.'

'No, we didn't, did we?' He actually smiled at the recollection. 'What was it she said, now?'

Esme remembered, but she wasn't about to help him out.

Not that she needed to, as he ran on, 'Ah, yes, having a degree from Oxford didn't make the cook's son any more eligible as a suitor to her daughters.'

Esme cringed at the memory, even though almost a decade had passed. She had sat at the long dining table, reduced to shocked silence by her mother's careless cruelty and watched the colour come and go in Jack's face, before pride had made him lash out.

She'd never before or since seen her mother so dumbstruck. But no one else had ever called her a dimwitted, mean-spirited, stuck-up cow.

Considering the anger that had made Jack Doyle's mouth a tight white line and the temper that had flashed in stormy grey eyes, it had been a fairly restrained response. The slamming of doors behind him had conveyed better his temper.

Her mother had sat red-faced at the head of the table while her sister Arabella had appeared from the adjoining room, sniggering with amusement.

It had been more than Esme could bear.

A decade on, she shut her eyes, expelling the scene from her mind before the camera could roll further.

'Still, there were consolations,' he added under his breath.

But loud enough for Esme to hear, to open her eyes again and meet his, to see the soft amusement in them.

She held his gaze for just a moment, then looked away, unable to stop her cheeks from flushing. He probably took it for remembered pleasure rather than the deep embarrassment it was.

A night with the wrong sister. Consolation prize of sorts. His behaviour understandable enough, but hers? Too desperate for words.

She buried the memory once more and took refuge in being brusque and businesslike. 'Talk to my mother if you choose... That's all the rooms except the attics and kitchens. Do you wish to see those?'

'Not particularly,' he responded. 'I have the attic dimensions and I probably know the kitchen layout better than you do yourself, young Miss Esme.'

He pretended to touch his forelock. It seemed like humour but Esme wasn't fooled. There was bitterness behind it, too. And why not?

But Esme refused to go on the defensive and muttered in agreement, 'Probably,' before walking ahead of him out onto the galleried landing and down the once magnificent staircase, now creaking with age.

She started to walk towards the front door but his voice halted her. 'Wouldn't it be easier to go through the kitchens to view the outbuildings?'

'You want to see those?' Esme frowned darkly. Surely he knew the layout of the rear yard, too.

'The state of them,' he confirmed. 'The stables weren't in great shape the last time I saw them.'

It could have been an innocent comment.

Perhaps only she remembered exact details of where and how.

But it made her both angry and embarrassed; she turned away before he could observe either emotion.

Her heels clicked on the marble floor as she stalked ahead, a tall, willowy creature with an erect back, and Jack followed, puzzling as to how he'd upset her this time.

He went over what he'd said. Nothing much. Just about the state of the stables the last time he'd seen them.

Ah! He recalled literally the last time. The night he'd woken up to Arabella and her little games and ended up spending part of it with her sister. Not his finest hour, whichever way you looked at it, so he tended not to look at it.

There wasn't much he could say now, either, so he said nothing.

She led the way outside into the back courtyard, a large square flanked by walls and the stable blocks. It was as he remembered only in a considerably worse state of repair. Grass and weeds were growing between cobblestones and someone had left piles of garden rubbish in one corner.

An old car, seemingly abandoned but actually belonging to Esme, stood rusting in one corner, and the red paint on garage and stable doors was cracked and peeling.

Esme had grown used to the decay of what had used to be kept immaculate while her father was alive, but she saw it afresh through Jack Doyle's eyes. She waited for him to make some derogatory remark, with every intention of snapping his head off if he did.

But he kept his thoughts to himself as he crossed the yard to the stable block. He went from stall to stall, eyes measuring, assessing, judging how much of the stone structure would have to be rebuilt.

Esme followed along, hovering at a distance, there to answer questions but wearing an expression that discouraged any. She supposed she should be trying to sell the place but she still doubted he was there to buy it.

He reached the tack room and found it locked. 'Have you the key?'

'No, it's back at—' she broke off abruptly, about to say the cottage, and switched to, 'Back at the house,' then added a suitably vague, 'Somewhere,' in case he asked her to produce it.

Not that there was anything incriminating inside the tack room. Just some odd pieces of bridle equipment. It was the mention of the cottage she'd been avoiding, although, on reflection, he might not have associated it with *the* cottage, originally his, now hers and Harry's.

He shrugged and moved on to the barn adjacent where they'd kept the feed. It was empty apart from some old hay in the loft, so it had been left open.

He went inside. Esme made no attempt to follow. She heard him moving around and waited, teeth gritted once more as she prepared for any possible remark he might pass, any allusion to the interlude they'd shared—impromptu passion fuelled by a bottle of whisky.

Her face flamed for the umpteenth time that afternoon. At twenty-six, she thought she'd grown out of blushing, but it seemed this humiliating habit from younger days had returned with a vengeance.

The Beetroot, that was another of Arabella's names for her. How she would cringe when Arabella called her that in company. In fact, she had cringed her way through a lot of her childhood and had been more than happy to grow up and grow out of these afflictions.

Now here she was, reverting at the rate of knots just because a ghost from the past had suddenly returned to haunt her.

Well, that was it. No more. She wasn't going to stand here like a spare part, waiting for Mr Jack Doyle to make some oblique crack that would complete her journey back in time.

She retreated to the house, leaving him to his own devices.

She entered the kitchen and, in pressing need of a cooling drink, opened the fridge. It was bare except for a few bottles of white wine, some tonic water and a tray of ice in the freezer compartment.

She'd been hoping for orange juice but the tonic was to be expected. It went with the gin bottle she took out of hiding from behind a food processor. She pursed her lips. Gin and tonic, her mother's favourite tipple. At one time more than a tipple, and, even now, her mother didn't seem to go through a day without at least a couple of stiff drinks.

Esme splashed some of the tonic in the bottom of a glass, added some ice but gave the gin a miss, having no inclination to follow her mother's example.

She picked up the glass, resting its chill against her forehead for a moment to cool herself down, before taking a swig just as Jack Doyle reappeared.

He walked quietly for a big man, coming to a halt in the kitchen doorway; his eyes switched from her face to the gin bottle on the worktop and back again.

Esme could almost hear his thoughts as he jumped to the wrong conclusions.

She decided to brazen it out. 'Do you want a drink?'

'Bit early for me,' he answered, 'but don't let me stop you.'

'I won't,' Esme muttered, rather than go into a denial that probably wouldn't be believed.

A long-drawn-out pause followed before he asked, 'How long have you been drinking?'

Esme, who had been studying the tonic in her glass, glanced up in time to catch his expression, a condescending blend of pity and disapproval. She wouldn't have liked it even if she'd had a drink problem.

She made a show of looking at her watch. 'About three minutes and twenty-five seconds.'

'I meant in the longer term.'

'I know.'

Esme pulled a face. He ignored it, his eyes resting on her with patient forbearance.

'Well?'

She wondered what he was expecting. A full and frank confession: My name is Esme and I'm an alcoholic.

'For the record, this is just tonic water.' The sheer nerve of him made her reckless. 'However, I had my first real drink at sixteen. Whisky, it was. Can't quite remember who supplied it.'

Except she remembered only too well who'd supplied the whisky. She wondered if he did, though.

She rather thought he did as the pitying look in his eyes became something else. Guilt? Distaste? Whichever, it served him right for coming over all sanctimonious.

But if she assumed he'd dropped the whole subject, she was mistaken.

'You were seventeen, as I recall,' he said instead.

For a moment she thought he was being pedantic, then she realised from his tone that her age was important to him. It had been at the time, too. That's why she'd lied.

No need to now. No need to tell him, either, only some devil inside her wanted to. Probably something to do with him attempting to take the moral high ground.

'A couple of weeks over sixteen, actually,' she corrected.

His eyes met hers, trying to sort out fact and fiction. 'You said—'

'Does it matter?' She saw it did to him, but the whole incident had suddenly lost its embarrassment factor—and romantic haze—for her. 'You were drunk, I was drunk, we both wanted to stick it to my mother. End of story.'

Esme knew she sounded a little crude, but that was better than blushing like a ninny. Anyway, as a version of events, it was close enough.

Jack gave a brief laugh. Out of relief, he suspected. He'd always felt guilty about the way he'd used Arabella's little sister but it seemed he'd underestimated her.

'Nothing like telling it how it is,' he commented at length. 'Still, you were always the most honest of the bunch... So no hard feelings?'

He approached her, hand outstretched.

Esme stared at this token of—of friendship, reconciliation, what exactly? She shrank from him in obvious distaste.

Unused to this reaction from women, Jack was more puzzled than anything else. She was treating him like a pariah but nothing he remembered in their past relationship warranted that. Sure, she'd been young—too young perhaps—when they'd made love that time, but she'd been willing. Very, as he recalled now.

He dropped his hand away. 'Isn't it rather late to treat me as untouchable?' he drawled with slight overtones of the American accent he'd picked up from years spent in California.

'Better late than never,' Esme retorted rather tritely and, almost hemmed into a corner, tried to brush past him.

He caught her bare arm, detaining her. 'If it's an apology you want, then you can have one. I was sorry, I *am* sorry, for the way I treated you.'

He sounded sincere and Esme was slightly disarmed by the fact. Easiest to reply in kind but she couldn't. Her stomach was clenching and unclenching at the touch of his hand on her skin. She put it down to revulsion and wondered when love had turned to hate. Some time over the last ten years? Or just today, when reality had caught up with her?

'I don't want anything from you,' she stated scornfully, 'so if you let my arm go, I'll show you out.'

Jack's eyes narrowed on her, analytical in their intent. She'd dismissed his apology and discounted their brief liaison as a moment of drunkenness, yet she was so angry her body was shaking with it.

'Let me go!' An order this time as she tried to wrest her arm away.

Jack held her fast. 'Not yet. Explain first.'

'Explain?' she echoed.

'Ten years ago,' he recalled, 'we parted on a more intimate note. OK, possibly assisted by some rather potent whisky. In the interim we have had no communication apart from one unanswered letter yet somehow I've become beneath contempt in your eyes... Well, call me slow, but I feel I've missed something.'

So had Esme. What unanswered letter?

'Or is it just the old class thing,' he continued at her silence, 'and us stable boys are fine for a quick session in the hayloft but not welcome up at the big house?'

'That's ridiculous!' Esme found the voice to protest at this absurdity. She hadn't been a snob at sixteen and she wasn't one now.

'Is it?' he challenged.

'Yes!' she almost spat back. 'For a start you were never a stable boy. All right, you mucked out occasionally to earn some pocket money but as often as not you got me to do it. Shovelling horse manure was far too menial for Mr Brainbox Doyle.'

'OK, maybe I wasn't in the literal sense,' he conceded, 'but I was low enough on the social ladder for you to look down your nose.'

'I didn't!' she could claim with angry conviction. 'In fact, if anything, you condescended to me. Poor, stupid, plain Midge, let's pat her on the head once in a while, be kind to her—that's when we're not treating her as invisible, of course.'

'I don't remember it being like that.'

'*You* wouldn't!'

Jack was surprised to find himself now on the defensive. 'I certainly never suggested you were plain or stupid.'

'You didn't have to,' she accused, 'it was bloody obvious. And, anyway, maybe I *was* plain and stupid!'

'No, you weren't.' Jack gave her a concerned look, as if now doubting her stability. 'You were pretty and funny and—'

'*Don't!*' Esme cut short this list of her qualities. 'You're patting me on the head again and I don't need it. I'm quite happy with myself and my life now. I am simply pointing out that any reluctance to be pawed by you at this precise moment in time has no connection with the social class into which we were born.'

'*Pawed?*' Clearly oscillating between amusement and annoyance, he lifted her arm by the wrist. 'This comes under the category of pawing?'

'I... Don't change the subject!' Esme snapped back.

'I'm afraid I've kind of lost it,' he admitted, 'but if this is what you consider pawing, you must have one pretty tame private life. Now if I'd done this—' an arm curved round her waist to draw her closer '—or this,' the other rose so a hand could briefly cup her cheek before turning to gently trail his knuckles down the long, elegant nape of her neck, 'Then I think you might be justified.'

He'd moved in on her so suddenly, Esme was too startled to react. By the time she did, the brief embrace was over and he'd actually let her go.

She was left with a heart racing like a train and a rage inside her that she could barely contain.

In fact, she didn't contain it, didn't even try. She let her hand come up, open-palmed, and slapped him as hard as she could. Slapped him so hard his head jerked backwards and her palm stung.

Esme watched as his cheek reddened, initial exhilaration giving way to horror. She'd never slapped anyone before, never felt the urge to. It was basic and primitive. Like sex.

Like his reaction. Shock quickly followed by retaliation as he grabbed her arms and, pushing them behind her back, trapped her against the kitchen cupboards. Then a hand was thrust in her hair, pulling her head back, leaving her just time to spit out a swear word before he covered her mouth with his.

It was an assault of lips and teeth that robbed her of breath but not the will to fight. She clutched at his jacket, trying to push him off, feeling fury not fear as she recognised this subjugation for what it was.

Only he was stronger and fury was dangerously akin to passion as the kiss went relentlessly on, demanding a response, forcing long-dormant feelings to the surface. There was no exact point when things changed and the hands digging into his chest began to uncurl and flatten and spread upwards to his shoulders. No dividing line between the hateful bruising of his mouth on hers and the sweet, sensual invasion that followed.

All she knew was that what she started off repudiating, she ended up silently begging for, as she slid her hands round his neck and held his mouth to hers, shifting in his arms until she could feel his heart beating against the softness of her breasts, and she moaned aloud as the hand circling her waist slipped lower, half lifting her body to his, already hard with arousal.

When he finally broke off, it was to catch breath and ask, with his deep silent gaze, for what he might merely have taken.

For a moment Esme hovered between madness and sanity, dizzy with desire yet shaken by the very force of it. So easily she could have let herself be swept away but somehow, through fear of drowning, she clawed her way back to the bank.

She didn't hit him again or play the outraged virgin or even pretend distaste. Half-ashamed, wholly disturbed, she said simply, 'I can't. I just can't. Please leave me alone.'

Quiet words, but shot with desperation, and more effective than any shouting, it seemed.

'Very well,' was all he muttered back as, releasing her completely, he pushed a distracted hand through his hair.

No argument. No pleading. She could have seen it as insulting how quickly he retreated, making for the hallway, his footsteps an echo on the marble, then gone, the front door closed quietly behind him.

But she saw nothing because her eyes were filling with tears at the raw, ragged pain from the scarred-over wound he'd reopened.

CHAPTER TWO

ESME didn't cry for long. It was an indulgence she could not afford. It was now mid-afternoon and soon she would have to go to pick up Harry.

She washed her face in cold water from the kitchen tap, trying to take the heat from it, then put the tonic and ice tray back in the fridge. She pushed the offending gin bottle back in its corner, half wishing she had taken a drink. At least then she could have blamed the alcohol for her pathetic behaviour.

It wasn't as though she was entirely unprepared for Jack Doyle's reappearance in her life. In fact, she'd imagined just such a scenario. Only in her version he would have changed, would not be so good-looking or smart or superior to most other men. She would wonder what she'd ever seen in him and be remote and dignified. Gone would be the young girl's infatuation with an older boy, because she was no longer a young girl.

Reality, of course, had made a mockery of all her imaginings. He hadn't changed, still maddeningly cool and collected ninety-nine per cent of the time, and frighteningly passionate that other one. And her? Well, it seemed she was still a walkover even if the puppy love had festered into resentment.

Or maybe it was as he'd implied: her private life was too tame. Could that be the reason? It had been a while—a long while, it seemed—since her last abortive relationship had made celibacy an attractive option.

Yes, that had to be it. Sex-starved after three years of abstinence, she might have kissed any personable man in the same circumstances.

It didn't say much for her self-restraint but she rather liked it as an explanation. In fact, she almost managed to convince herself of its truth. She would have but for the image of Charles Bell Fox, the nearest thing she currently had to a boyfriend. She'd known him for ever, liked him always and, encouraged by her mother, had even recognised him as good husband material. Yet she had repelled all his gentle overtures.

But then Charles was a gentleman. He'd never kiss her against her will, never force physical intimacy until some base sexual urges kicked in. Perhaps if he had, they might have progressed further than their current careful friendship.

A perverse thought, she shook her head, and, checking that Jack Doyle and his undoubtedly expensive motor had disappeared from the drive, locked and bolted the front door, before keying in the burglar-alarm code on the box above the cellar steps.

She exited smartly via the kitchen to the courtyard, then beyond to the back service road through the woods, passing her current home.

Intended originally for an unmarried gamekeeper, and built in the late 1890s, it wasn't a pretty cottage, the stone roughly hewn and with ramshackle outhouses tacked on. But Esme had done her best to improve the outside with a bright terracotta masonry paint and bold blue doors and an array of pots and baskets of flowers to distract from the random ugliness of the house. She doubted Jack Doyle would have recognised it as *his* old home.

She slipped inside for a moment to collect a denim jacket and change her heels to flats. Transformed instantly from fashionable woman-about-town to young practical mother, she didn't bother locking her door as she set off along a short cut through the wood to the rear gates of the estate.

She glanced at her watch, and, though on time, she quickened her pace. It was always an anxiety—that one day the bus would arrive early and deposit Harry alone at the side of the road.

The high wrought-iron gates were locked, so she used the door in the wall, its key hidden behind loose stonework. She emerged onto the verge of the main road and only then did she observe the car parked on the far side.

It was a sleek dark green auto, built on racing lines; she

didn't recognise the make or number and, with the inside obscured by tinted glass, it was impossible to see the driver. But she knew all the same. Who else would be sitting opposite the rear gates to Highfield when there was nothing else of interest on this back road?

He had to have spotted her, too, so no point in scuttling back inside. It would smack of panic and fear, and, besides, the bus was due to arrive. She could only stand there and pray he would tire of staring at two rusting locked gates and a six-foot-high stone wall.

Under her breath she muttered the word, 'Go,' over and over, as if she could will him to leave, and believed the spell had worked when she heard his engine start up.

She cheered too early, however, as he pulled out onto the road and executed a 180-degree turn to bring his car alongside her.

The driver's window slid silently downwards and Esme wasn't certain if she would prefer it to be him or a total stranger lurking for nefarious purposes.

She opted for the total stranger at about the same second as Jack Doyle offered her one of his slightly crooked smiles.

'Waiting for someone?' he enquired.

A 'no' formed on her lips but thankfully she never got round to uttering it. Because why else would she possibly be here, standing at the roadside?

She limited herself to a nod.

'Not very reliable, are they,' he suggested, 'leaving you out here on your own? Anyone could come along.'

Fake concern? Had to be.

It prompted Esme to retaliate with a dry, 'They already have.'

A jibe he ignored as he ran on, 'I'll give you a lift to wherever you're going.'

She was surprised into a passing polite, 'No, thanks.'

'All right, suit yourself.' He shrugged. 'I'll just hang around until he comes.'

'No, you mustn't!' Esme didn't have to feign horror at the idea.

He looked at her curiously. 'Jealous type?'

He had the wrong idea, totally, but Esme didn't disabuse him. The important thing was for him to be gone by the time the bus arrived.

'Yes, yes, he is,' she agreed. 'I mean really. He'll be here any second and if he sees you...'

Esme glanced fearfully down the road and left him to fill in the rest.

He did so with darkening brow. 'Is that why you were so upset when I kissed you?'

Esme nodded. It was too good an excuse to waste. In fact, a little embellishment wouldn't go amiss.

'He's very possessive. Doesn't like me even speaking to other men. So please, Jack, just go.' She trained appealing blue eyes on him.

Jack saw traces of the old Esme and was torn. He suddenly felt responsible for her, certain that any man so possessive had to be bad news. But then what right had he to interfere? He had been away too long.

'Please,' Esme repeated with genuine urgency as she heard the bus in the distance.

'Yes, all right.' He remained a moment longer, holding her anxious gaze, then, putting the car into gear, roared off along the highway.

If Esme felt guilty, she also felt justified as the bus came into view, passing Jack going in the opposite direction. Talk about close calls.

'What's wrong?' Harry asked as she practically pulled him off the bus and hustled him through the door in the wall.

'Nothing.' She just didn't trust Jack not to change his mind and return.

Because that was something else she remembered about him. How protective he'd been at times, looking out for her when she'd been hurt, physically and emotionally. Her hero until he'd proved otherwise.

'So how was school?' She tried to sound normal to Harry and it came out forced.

Her son frowned before shrugging. 'The same.'

'And those boys?' This time genuine worry.

He pulled a face.

Esme interpreted that as bad. 'Look, if you'll let me go into school—'

'No,' Harry cut across her, 'you mustn't, Mum. You'll just make it worse.'

Perhaps he was right. Esme could see his point. Having your mother go wading in on your behalf to complain about Dwayne and Dean, the twins from hell—or at least the roughest housing estate in Southbury—wasn't going to do his street cred much good, but she felt so helpless.

'OK, OK.' She put an arm round his shoulder and gave it a squeeze. 'But if it escalates, you must tell me.'

He gave a brief nod.

Unsure if he understood, Esme added, 'By escalate, I mean—'

'I know, Mum,' he cut in once more. 'If they threaten me with an AK47, I have to tell you, right?'

He gave her a wry smile and she smiled back, although hardly reassured.

'I realise you're joking, Harry,' she ran on, 'but do any of the boys carry weapons—penknives, say?'

He shrugged again before saying, 'They're not allowed.'

That hardly answered the question, either. His junior school, City Road, had a nicely printed booklet of rules and mission statements on bullying, but that hadn't stopped her son becoming the target for boys in the year group above him.

Esme watched as he strode ahead of her now. Nothing visible could mark him down for derision. He was tall for his age and, to her eyes, a good-looking boy with a shock of blond hair and a thin, clever face, but no spectacles or physical weaknesses or strange mannerisms that would single him out.

The teacher had suggested the fault might lie elsewhere. In a school dominated by the local accent, Harry talked differently—in the same regionless precise English that had been encouraged by Esme's various boarding-schools. But that wasn't all. There was his cleverness, indisputable and hard to conceal. Harry had tried, very quickly learning not to put up his hand in class or work too hard or say anything to draw attention to it. But it was part of him, the way he was, self-contained and independent, able to absorb everything at a glance without conscious effort.

Esme had never been able to decide whether it was a curse or a blessing, but she didn't pride herself on it. She knew it didn't come from her.

Her contribution was his shock of blond hair and fair-skinned looks but otherwise he was someone else's child. It wasn't a striking likeness. It was there, however, in the eyes, solemnly grey to her sky-blue, and some of his expressions. There, if you cared to look. Enough to feel a need to keep him and his father apart.

When they reached the cottage, Harry immediately excused himself. He left his bag in the hall and went up to his room built into the attic space.

Esme knew he would be already logging on to his computer, his intellectual mainstay. She might have tried to stop him if she could have offered an alternative, but, without brothers or sisters or children to play with, it was difficult.

Her mother had suggested boarding-school more than once but Esme had neither the money nor the inclination to send Harry away, having hated boarding herself.

Besides, she couldn't imagine life without him. Not that it had been easy in the early years. She'd been a frightened teenager, back at school when she'd realised she might be pregnant. Morning sick, then simply sick with anxiety, she had actually lost weight, so her bump had gone unnoticed almost to the seventh month. Then discovery had been followed by disgrace and dispatch homewards.

Recriminations had given way to arrangements. A cousin of her mother's in Bath. Adoption at birth. Forget it ever happened.

Esme had gone along with it all up until a twenty-hour labour had thrust her rudely into adulthood. Everything had changed after that. She'd looked at her newborn son and, from somewhere, had found the courage to defy her mother's ultimatum: come home minus baby or don't come home at all.

Social Services had helped to get her into a mother and baby hostel. It had been a steep learning curve. On top of her new-found responsibility for a tiny human had come the shock of being out in the real world. She'd ceased feeling hard-done-by when she'd heard the other girls' stories. While they'd talked of bad-news boyfriends and abusive stepfathers and drunken mothers, her childhood had seemed a fairy story.

In the hostel she'd learned to cook and clean and wash; she'd also learned to curse and swear and stand up for herself. From there she'd moved to a flat in Bristol, ten flights up with a lift that rarely worked.

She'd stuck it out until a two-year-old Harry had fallen on the stairwell. A grazed knee—no big deal. But in the corner, inches from his hand, a discarded syringe.

It was at that point she'd swallowed her pride and taken the bus home. Her mother had been speechless for the first thirty seconds, barely recognising her younger daughter in this stick-thin, badly dressed young woman, then, drawing breath, she'd launched into a tirade of I-told-you-sos before eventually allowing Esme through the door.

In this respect Rosalind Scott-Hamilton had behaved pretty much as her daughter had anticipated. The true surprise had been her reaction to Harry. While bundled up in the pushchair and covered by a rain-hood he'd been an anonymous lump, but when he'd woken and climbed out of his pushchair to stand silently gazing at his grandmother it had appeared even she wasn't immune to his charm.

'What a perfectly beautiful little boy!' she'd exclaimed in utter surprise.

Esme hadn't known whether to be gratified or insulted. She'd certainly understood the implication—how could someone as ordinary as her younger daughter have produced such a son?

Still, it was Harry who had helped bridge the gap. Not that her mother acted the part of fond grandmother—she wouldn't even allow Harry to use the term—but there was an affection there that allowed her to ignore his ignominious start in life.

Thus, Esme had rejoined the fold, but only partly, setting up home in the cottage and trading some of her acquired domestic skills for petty cash from her mother until her twenty-first birthday had brought a small trust fund from her godmother.

It was hardly an exciting existence but she'd been content enough till today. Now it seemed under threat and she couldn't wait to phone her mother.

'Darling—' Rosalind Scott-Hamilton called most female acquaintances that, having lately taken on the persona of an ageing film star '—I was going to ring you tonight. How did it go, the viewing?'

Esme breathed deeply before ignoring the question and demanding instead, 'Mother, are you aware who the viewer was?'

'Who the viewer was?' Rosalind gave herself time to think. 'Some internet millionaire, I believe. Cash buyer, according to the agent. Why?'

'It's Jack Doyle,' Esme told her bluntly.

'Jack Doyle?' Her mother was clearly trawling through her memory for the name.

'Mrs Doyle's son,' Esme prompted.

'*Mrs Doyle!*' Her mother echoed this name, too.

Esme sighed heavily. 'Mrs Doyle. Our cook. Lived in the cottage.'

'Yes, yes,' Rosalind Scott Hamilton dismissed, 'I *do* know who Mrs Doyle is, or was. I was expressing surprise...Jack Doyle. Who'd have thought it? After all these years and in the market to buy Highfield... Did he say if he was inter-ested?'

'No, Mother, he didn't!' This conversation was not going how Esme had planned.

'Well, he must be,' her mother ran on. 'I mean, he knows what the place is like and it hasn't changed much from when he was a boy. The question is whether he can afford it—or was he just on a sentimental journey? Perhaps Robin can make a few enquiries in the City.'

The City was the heart of London's money markets from where her stepfather did his wheeling and dealing.

'But surely you wouldn't sell to Jack Doyle even if he was interested?' Esme appealed.

'Why not?'

'Well...all the things you said about him once.'

To her mother, Jack had been a jumped-up working-class boy who had dared to imagine himself suitable for one of her daughters just because he'd managed a first from Oxford.

'Things,' her mother muttered vaguely. 'Oh, you mean the time he fancied his chances with Arabella? Yes, that was quite absurd. Still, in hindsight, who knows? She might have been better off with him than that character she did marry.'

Esme was speechless for a moment. How the world had changed! Her mother had been absolutely delighted when Arabella had married Franklin Homer, supposed heir to an American banking fortune. Only the fortune seemed to have dissolved along with the marriage.

'Anyway,' her mother resumed, 'if Jack Doyle wants to buy Highfield, then good luck to him.'

Esme's heart sank. 'You can't mean that, Mother.'

'Whyever not?' An impatient edge crept into her mother's voice. 'I really am surprised at you, Esme. I would have thought you'd be delighted at the whole idea. You're the one who has always championed the underdog, maintained there is no fundamental difference between the working class and us, apart from money.'

Esme didn't know about 'championing' the underdog. She was usually too busy looking out for herself and Harry. But she had always deplored her mother's blatant snobbery.

'Anyway, I need the money,' her mother continued. 'You know that, darling. I've explained.'

Esme could have said, No, you don't. You have a husband as rich as sin. But her mother saw Highfield as her insurance policy in case anything happened to her second marriage.

'You're bound to sell it eventually,' Esme pointed out. 'You don't have to sell it to Jack Doyle.'

'No, but it would be simply perverse to turn down an offer from him,' Rosalind argued back. 'And I don't really see the problem. It's not as if you and Jack were ever involved.'

A silence followed. Esme could have broken it with the knowledge she'd always withheld from her mother, but she doubted it would change anything.

She changed tack instead. 'Well, at least make sure the estate agent clarifies what's included in the sale.'

'What do you mean, darling?'

Was it her imagination or did her mother sound cagey?

'He thinks the cottage is up for grabs. I told him it wasn't but he didn't believe me. Perhaps Connell, Richards & Baines could draw his attention to the fact?'

'Yes, well…' There was a pause while her mother decided on her phrasing.

'Mother?' Esme prompted with growing suspicion. 'You haven't changed your mind? You said I could have a life interest in the cottage.'

'I know, darling, and I meant it,' her mother claimed, 'but James Connell says it just isn't feasible, parcelling up the estate that way. But don't worry, you should be all right. You're a sitting tenant.'

Esme did not believe this. 'And if we're not all right, what do Harry and I do then?'

'Well, obviously you'd have to find somewhere else,' Rosalind sighed in reply, 'but would that be so awful? I mean, the cottage is very basic. Little better than staff quarters.'

'*We* like it,' Esme claimed, temper finally rising, 'and, compared to bed and breakfast accommodation for the homeless, it's palatial!'

'Don't be absurd, darling!' Rosalind snapped back. 'You have other alternatives.'

'Like?' Esme was confident that her mother wasn't about to invite Harry and her to live in her Kensington four-storey in London.

'I don't know,' Rosalind replied just as crossly. 'I'm sure

there are lots of places you could go, if you would stop playing the martyr... I've heard Charles Bell Fox would have you at the drop of a hat, and you could do a lot worse.'

Esme agreed. She could. But it was hardly any business of her mother's.

'Charles and I are just friends,' Esme could claim in perfect conscience.

'Only because you won't let the poor boy be anything else,' her mother countered, 'and goodness knows why. He's rich, he's eligible, he's even quite good-looking. What are you waiting for?'

'Nothing,' Esme replied tartly. 'I'll call him up now, shall I? Ask if he'd like us to shack up together?'

Her mother gave a weary sigh. 'Is that meant to be funny?'

'Not especially.'

'Because it isn't—and you know perfectly well I was talking about marriage, not cohabitation. I think you've already done enough of that, don't you?'

'What?' Esme was genuinely puzzled for a moment. She'd never lived with anyone other than her family. 'Oh, right, my fall from grace? I don't think casual sex counts as cohabitation, Mother.'

A loud tut came down the phone. At times her mother liked to pretend she was a prude.

'Really, Esme,' her mother reproved, 'it's nothing to be proud of—having a baby with someone you barely knew. What have you said to Charles about Harry?'

'Nothing.' Charles had scrupulously avoided the subject.

'Well, I trust when you do,' Rosalind continued, 'you'll dress it up a bit. Falling into bed with some Italian boy you met in a café sounds very loose.'

Esme controlled an errant desire to laugh. Such a lame story, it was a source of perennial wonder that her mother still believed it.

'OK, Mother, I'll bear it in mind,' Esme replied, tongue-in-cheek, 'when and if Charles ever asks me to marry him.'

'Good.' Her mother seemed oblivious of any irony. 'Because he really is your best bet. You certainly can't expect me to keep bailing you out... Now I really must go. I'm having people for dinner.'

Boiled or fried? Esme was tempted to ask, but was already holding a dead line. She replaced the receiver and pushed a worried hand through her hair before hearing a sound behind her.

She turned to find Harry standing on the open staircase from his bedroom. He looked vaguely troubled. How much had he overheard?

He stared at her briefly before saying, 'I'm hungry. What's for tea?'

A normal, ordinary-boy question. Esme allowed it to dispel her fears and led the way through to the kitchen as she declared, 'We have a choice: pizza, pizza or pizza.'

Harry rolled his eyes at this familiar joke but joined in by saying, 'OK, pizza. The second one.'

'That's pizza with pepperoni and olives,' she announced.

It elicited a boyish, 'Yuk. I've changed my mind. I'll have pizza, the first one.'

'Anchovies.'

'Double yuk.'

'Ham and mushroom?'

'Yeah, suppose that'll do.'

'But no picking off the mushroom,' she warned as she got the ready-made meal out of the freezer, 'and you'll have it with orange juice so at least something healthy passes your lips today.'

He pulled a face. 'I had chips for lunch. That's a vegetable.'

'Potatoes are a vegetable,' she corrected. 'Fry them and we're talking a whole new ballgame.'

'Like the difference between football and pinball,' he suggested wryly.

'Quite,' she agreed, wrestling with an oven shelf that refused to pull out.

The cooker was ancient. It had been here in the time of the Doyles and must have been antiquated then. A poor tool for a woman like Mary Doyle, who had been a wonderful cook.

A lovely person, too. Kind and thoughtful and endlessly patient. That was how Esme remembered her, anyway.

She'd died that same year, before Harry had been conceived, so she'd never seen her little grandson.

It was sad, really. Though her own mother wouldn't even let Harry call her grandmother, she imagined Mary Doyle would have been different.

Would she have told her? Esme suspected there would have been no need. She would have seen. The smile was Jack's, as was the temperament. Maybe it was elemental, a recognition of genes shared.

Thank God it hadn't been put to the test that afternoon. But what if Jack actually bought Highfield? Wouldn't a meeting of man and boy be inevitable?

She shook her head. Yes, it would, but it wasn't going to happen. It couldn't.

Esme had no logical reason for this certainty, just blind faith and the fact she couldn't allow herself to believe otherwise.

CHAPTER THREE

ESME dismissed the Doyles from her thoughts and concentrated on making tea, which they ate at the kitchen table.

Later, with Harry in bed and the cottage gravely silent, she tried to focus on her latest project. She'd been commissioned to design a master bedroom for a mock-Tudor house owned by a City dealer friend of her stepfather and his advertising-executive wife, but it was proving difficult as the two had quite conflicting ideas on what they wanted. Esme, who had fallen into interior design more by chance than planning, had come to accept the work required enormous tact and patience as well as flair and a good eye.

She pored over colour charts now, hoping for inspiration, but her mind kept wandering. Back to that summer almost ten years ago.

She'd come home for the holidays to find Jack there. He'd returned from Ireland to wait for the results of his finals and dispose of his mother's things. Her mother had allowed him to remain in the cottage, paying him subsistence money for gardening duties and general repairs.

It showed how little her mother had really known Jack. To her, he'd been the cook's son, and therefore suited to manual work. Esme, of course, had known him a lot better. He'd tutored her, ridden with her and babysat on more than one occasion. Undoubtedly strong and fit, he, nevertheless, had not been handyman material. Give him the intricacies of a computer to fathom, and he'd be your man. Give him a stable door off its hinges and he'd be resolutely uninterested.

He'd put in the hours—mowing the lawns on the ride-on tractor, feeding the two horses left in the stables, washing down cars and the yard—but no more.

Esme had watched from a distance, wishing she could keep

him company as she had so many times before. But something had changed. Him or her or the situation.

It wasn't that she'd had nothing to say to him. On the contrary, she had longed to go up and ask him how he was and tell him how much she, too, missed his mother. It had just seemed that the gap between them—social, age, intelligence—had grown into a chasm since the Christmas when they'd last talked.

Or maybe it had been Arabella. She'd been home, too, from the Swiss finishing-school that had been meant to teach her to be a lady but had, to Esme's mind, failed miserably. Bored and kicking her heels while a socially acceptable job was being found for her in London, she had looked for a way to kill time and settled on Jack.

At first Esme hadn't worried. Jack had always been offhand to Arabella and at times obliquely rude.

Esme wondered sometimes if that was why she'd become infatuated. All her life she'd played second fiddle to Arabella, with Jack the only one seeming to prefer her.

Until that summer, of course, when August brought a heatwave and with it a kind of madness.

Or maybe it had just been sex.

She'd felt it, too. Weak at the knees every time Jack had come near. Tongue-tied and pathetic whenever he'd smiled her way. Morose with her awkwardness. Shot through with jealousy as his thing with Arabella had developed.

She would have borne it better if Arabella had been discreet. But that had been the whole point. Arabella had wanted her to know she was sleeping with 'the stable boy,' as she'd referred to Jack, and, in doing so, had made it plain she was just amusing herself.

Even then it had been Jack Esme bled for, so much so that she'd felt compelled to tell him the truth.

'I know about you and Arabella,' she declared, only to be fixed by one of his emotionless stares. 'I don't want to interfere or anything.'

'Then don't,' he advised, almost curtly.

It hurt. Jack never talked to her like that. Not normally.

She couldn't stop. She didn't want to see him hurt in turn. 'I just wondered if you realised,' she ran on determinedly, 'that she's not serious about…well, about you and her.'

He looked annoyed, more than annoyed, although he responded in a kind of joke. 'So don't go buying any engagement rings, is that it?'

'Something like that.' She nodded.

His eyes narrowed further on her grave face, assessing her motives, before he chose to laugh back. 'Don't worry, I've still got the receipt.'

'What?' It took Esme a moment to understand. 'Oh, right.' Another joke…or was it?

'The question is, who's put you up to this pep talk?' he considered aloud. 'Your lovely sister or the family matriarch?'

'Who?'

'Your mother.'

'Oh.' Esme was made to feel dense. 'No, nobody. I just thought… Never mind.'

She decided it would be impossible to explain why she was concerned without exposing her own feelings.

He was already looking at her in a funny way, and she could feel colour ebb and flow in her cheeks.

'Forget I said anything,' she urged instead.

'OK, I will.' He echoed her tone but a suspicion of a smile was lurking at the corners of his mouth.

No longer cross with her. Just amused. Was that better or worse?

Worse, maybe. It certainly added to her mortification and, turning, she walked away.

He called to her, 'Midge, wait up.' But, in response, she quickened her footsteps until she'd broken into a run, fleeing back to the house and the sanctuary of her bedroom.

After that, she couldn't bear to face him or Arabella—she imagined him relaying the conversation to her—and became a virtual recluse, skulking in her room apart from at mealtimes.

The incident at dinner happened a week later. To Esme, it

came out of the blue. Not, it seemed, to her mother or Arabella.

When Jack called at the front door—a first—the new cook was instructed to show him into the dining room.

Arabella disappeared through an interconnecting door and her mother instructed Esme, 'Stay silent.'

So she did, silent and forgotten at one end of the table.

Jack barely glanced her way. 'You changed the lock,' he directed at their mother. 'What did you think I was going to do? Smash the place up?'

'For all I know,' Rosalind Scott-Hamilton sniffed back, 'you're capable of it… Now you've been thwarted.'

'Thwarted?' Jack echoed. 'Meaning what exactly?'

'Meaning, young man—' from her sitting position her mother still managed to look down her nose '—your attempts to compromise my daughter have come to naught.'

'Compromise?' A ridiculously old-fashioned word, it was clear Jack thought so, too.

'But in case you've failed to get the message—' her mother paused briefly before launching into a vituperative speech, making it crystal clear that Jack wasn't fit to court her eldest daughter.

As Arabella was listening in the next room—and Arabella was quite capable of defying their mother and interrupting— Esme assumed this tirade had her approval.

Esme watched the anger darkening Jack's brow, heard his intake of breath, then cheered silently as he finally retaliated to her mother's snobbery with a few well-chosen words.

When he turned on his heel and slammed the door behind him, her mother still had her mouth hanging open.

Esme pushed back her chair to follow.

'And where are you going?' Her mother turned on her.

'To my room.' She could hardly say, After Jack.

Her mother might have insisted she stay, but when Arabella reappeared the focus of her attention shifted.

'Yes, all right.' She waved Esme away.

Esme knew she was already forgotten and could please herself. She hurried to the front door, imagining Jack had exited the same way he'd entered, but there was no sign of anyone in the drive. She retraced her steps, creeping past the dining room *en route* to the kitchen.

The new cook, Maggie, was putting the finishing touches to dessert. She glanced up at Esme, noted her expression, then gestured towards the back door.

'He's gone to the barn.'

'The barn?'

Maggie nodded. 'I gave him a bottle to keep out the chill.'

'A bottle? A bottle of what?'

'Whisky from the larder. I'll replace it, of course.'

Esme wasn't worried about that, but frowned. 'Jack doesn't drink.'

Maggie shook her head—over Esme's *naïveté*. 'All men drink. Trust me… He'll need it tonight, too, if he's to sleep in the hayloft.'

'But why…?' Esme was still trying to catch up with events.

'He has nowhere else,' Maggie relayed. 'Your mother's dumped his stuff and had a locksmith in. It seems she didn't like him and your sister being so friendly.'

Esme had gathered as much but why now, so suddenly? Arabella had been hanging round Jack for weeks and her mother had done little to prevent it, being indulgent in the extreme to her elder daughter.

'I fetched this down earlier—' Maggie indicated a blanket draped over a chair '—but he's gone off without it.'

'I'll take it to him.' Esme picked it up.

'Are you sure?' Maggie looked a little uncertain but didn't try to stop Esme, adding, 'I'll leave the door on the latch.'

'Thanks.' Esme went out into the night.

It was almost nine, but, being summer, it was still light as Esme crossed the stable yard to the barn at the end.

The door squeaked on rusty hinges; she called out, 'Jack,' faintly at first, then louder at his lack of response.

'Up here.' Reluctantly admitted, it came from the hayloft above.

Esme stepped fully inside. Very little light filtered into the barn but she knew her way by memory. She reached the ladder and started to climb, pushing the blanket up before her. She was hardly attired for the occasion, in a summer dress, but she stayed poised at the top while her eyes adjusted to the semi-darkness.

'It's me, Esme.' She identified herself in case he'd hoped for someone different.

His voice came from the far wall and sounded gruffer than usual. 'I know it's you. What do you want?'

'I—I...' What did she want? To tell him she was sorry, she supposed. It suddenly seemed inadequate and his tone was scarcely welcoming.

'Well, while you're deciding,' he mocked her stammering, 'either come up or go down before you fall and break your neck.'

A torch was switched on and shone across the floor so she had some light to guide her. She still couldn't see him but it was obvious he was indifferent as to whether she stayed or went.

Esme hovered for a moment longer, then scrambled all the way into the hayloft, ripping the hem of her dress. Uncaring, she edged nearer on all fours until she reached the back wall.

She handed over the blanket but didn't get too close to him. She sensed he wouldn't like it.

A brief, 'Thanks,' was uttered.

She stole a glance in his direction but his face was in shadow and, when she was at rest, he switched off the torch, saying, 'The batteries are almost dead.'

'Oh, right.' Feeling inadequate, Esme wondered what to say next.

She could make out a bulging rucksack on one side of him. All his worldly possessions were in that? She wanted to tell him how unfair she thought it all, but he clearly wasn't inclined to talk.

She heard the rustle of a sleeve as he lifted an arm, then the sound of him drinking.

She'd never seen him drink alcohol. She wasn't seeing him now, either, but she took Maggie's word about the whisky.

She shivered and, in a spirit of recklessness, said, 'Can I have some of that?'

'I don't think so,' he replied. 'You're not legal age yet, are you?'

'I'm eighteen,' she claimed.

'Seventeen, more like,' he countered.

'All right, seventeen.'

Esme settled for that. Sixteen would seem barely out of childhood to a man of twenty-two and she desperately wanted to be older for him.

'I've drunk it before.'

'Really.'

'I have,' she insisted, 'at boarding-school. The girls are always drinking.'

'Among other things,' he muttered, more to himself than her. 'Well, I'd give you a sip to stop your teeth chattering, but your bitch of a mother might accuse me of corrupting the second of her daughters.'

'You didn't corrupt Arabella.' Esme was conscious of some disloyalty to her sister but it was the truth. Arabella had made no secret of the fact she'd been sleeping with boys for years.

'I am aware of that,' he laughed harshly.

'But you still liked her,' Esme observed aloud.

He assumed it was a question and he shrugged in reply. 'I'm not sure liking came into it.'

'Oh.' Esme concluded from this that it was a much stronger emotion he'd felt.

They lapsed into silence. It wasn't companionable. Esme just didn't know what to say next. She'd come tearing after him, distressed by the way her family had treated him, wanting somehow to make up for it. But she understood that Jack would feel no better if she started leaking sympathy over him.

She began to shiver in earnest. The barn was unheated and the only window was wood-shuttered, a draught coming in through the cracks. She tried to keep warm by hugging herself.

'Here.' He handed her the bottle while he shrugged out of

the denim jacket he was wearing and draped it over her shoulders, followed by the blanket across her legs.

'Thanks.' She was instantly warmer. Heat from his body was trapped in the material.

She found she was still holding the bottle and took a swig from it. By force of will she managed to avert a coughing fit as the liquid burnt the back of her throat. Till then her sole alcohol consumption had been the occasional glass of white wine. This was much more potent stuff, the taste horrible but the effects magically calming.

She handed the whisky back to him and he wiped the top of the bottle before taking another swig.

'So where exactly was Arabella?' he asked her.

'I…um…' Esme wondered whether the truth was a good idea.

'In the next room?' he suggested.

She started with surprise. 'Why do you think that?'

'I'm right, aren't I?' he concluded. 'Pressing her shell-like to the door, no doubt.'

Esme stared in his direction, but it was too gloomy in here to make out his expression. His tone didn't tell her much either. He sounded angry rather than heartbroken.

'If you knew she was there,' she said puzzled, 'why didn't you say anything?'

He shrugged. 'Let her have her fun.'

'I don't understand,' Esme admitted.

'No,' he agreed, but didn't enlighten her.

She sensed he considered her too young to comprehend the complexities of adult relationships. He was wrong, however. She certainly understood her own feelings, a blend of jealousy, sympathy and passion.

It was jealousy that had her asking, 'Is this where you used to meet, you and Arabella?'

'To do the dirty deed, you mean?' He didn't spare her blushes. Not that he could see them in the gloom. 'Hardly. Your sister would have a screaming fit if a spider so much as touched her leg.'

Esme concluded they must have used the house, but had suddenly lost her appetite for further details.

'I don't suppose you'd believe that we didn't actually do anything,' he remarked at length.

'No.' Esme didn't like being taken for a fool. 'Do we have to talk about this?'

He glanced towards her and she could imagine his brow rising. After all, she'd started the conversation.

But he let it go with a brief, 'Not as far as I'm concerned,' and raised the bottle back to his lips.

Esme assumed it was to anaesthestise himself from feeling.

'Do you drink a lot?' she asked.

He choked a little at this bold question, then laughed shortly. 'Only on special occasions.'

And this was one? Esme didn't see it. She took it for sarcasm.

'Do you?' he added.

'Me?'

'Drink a lot?'

He was teasing. At six years older than her, he thought he had the right. But condescension was the last thing Esme wanted from him.

'Depends what you call a lot.' She was studiously casual. 'Weekends mostly. There are always bottles of something knocking around at school. The girls take them from home.'

It was true enough. Some of the girls at boarding-school were almost hardened drinkers, having started stealing their parents' liquor from quite a young age. She tended to avoid that crowd, however.

'And there was me,' he drawled back, 'thinking it was all midnight feasts and jolly hockey sticks for you rich types.'

Rich types? He'd never called her that before. But then her family had never called him a 'common oik' until tonight.

'What about men?'

'Men?'

'Boys,' he qualified. 'Do they figure in these drunken orgies?'

His voice was laced with amusement. He obviously still thought her a kid, playing at being a grown-up.

With a mind to shock, she said, 'Deering College is just a mile away. We meet their boys in our sports pavilion. That's where *we* do the dirty deed.'

She quoted him, able to sound convincing because it was all true. *She* just wasn't one of the 'we' that did it. Sure, she had kissed a few boys at school dances, even allowed a little touching over clothes, but nothing else.

A silence followed while he decided if he believed her. 'It seems I've misjudged you, little Midge,' he eventually commented.

What did that mean? He'd thought her a nice girl before, now he didn't?

'I'm not a slag or anything, though,' she added, blushing in the darkness.

'No, of course not.' His tone was mock-serious.

Esme kind of wished she hadn't started this either but, having embarked on her bad-girl image, felt obliged to maintain it.

'Can I have some more?' she asked after he took another drink.

'Is that a good idea?' He clearly didn't think so.

'I can take it,' she claimed.

'I'm not sure I can,' he laughed back. 'But as it is yours, filched from your larder...'

He extended the bottle to her.

This time she was prepared for the fire at the back of her throat and the unpleasant taste, if not the gradual lowering of inhibitions.

'Steady on,' he advised when she took a couple of long sips. 'I don't want to be carrying you home, even if it is only a couple of hundred yards to your back door.'

'You wouldn't manage it.' Esme knew she was a carthorse compared to her svelte sister.

'Probably not,' he conceded.

'Thanks,' she muttered, piqued.

'I was agreeing with you,' he pointed out.

'Well, I'd prefer you didn't,' she threw back.

'I don't think I understand women.' He reclaimed the bottle from her as she raised it back to her lips.

'Evidently not,' Esme muttered in retaliation.

'With reference to?' he enquired.

She'd been thinking about herself—how he still hadn't a clue about the way she felt.

It seemed wiser to say, 'Arabella.'

'Not one of my finer moments,' he conceded. 'I should have known what would happen. In fact, I'd have been better off if I had just slept with her.'

As opposed to what—falling in love?

Yet he didn't seem too devastated. More exasperated with himself. Or was that the recuperative powers of the whisky?

It certainly had a strange effect on a person, as Esme answered bitchily, 'Everyone else has.'

'Quite,' he agreed, laughing.

Not the reaction she'd expected at all. She was sure she didn't understand men.

'About the cottage—' she switched subjects '—I don't imagine my mother can just throw you out like that. There must be laws. You could find a solicitor. I have some money if—'

'No, forget it!' He stopped her speaking by squeezing her hand. 'You're a good kid, Esme, but there's no need. I was leaving, anyway. I have a job in the States.'

'I...I...' Esme felt as if she'd just been kicked.

'I assumed Arabella would have told you.'

No, nothing. But, to be fair, Esme couldn't bear to talk about Jack with Arabella.

'Wh-when are you coming back?' she finally managed.

'I'm not,' he declared. 'Not here, anyway. Nothing to come back for now.'

There's me, Esme longed to say, but he would have thought her mad. Perhaps she was. She'd spent endless hours dreaming of the day Jack Doyle would suddenly notice her. Open his eyes, see beyond puppy fat and teenage gaucheness and realise she was the one. Now, in an instant, all those dreams dissolved into dust.

She struggled for words, anything to fill the silence so he couldn't hear *her* heart beating in distress.

'I have to go.' She didn't care if it seemed abrupt.

She pushed away from the wall on which they were both leaning.

'Here's your jacket.' She shrugged out of the denim and made to get to her feet.

'Wait up!' He caught her arm and she lost momentum, coming back to rest on her knees.

'That hurt!' she complained, a cover for her real feelings.

He ignored it. 'Look, I'm sorry if I've upset you—'

'You haven't!' Esme denied, but her tone gave her away.

That and her distraught look as he switched on the torch once more.

'I would have told you but...' He searched for a reason.

There was none, of course. Why should he tell *her*?

'But I'm nobody,' she said it for him. 'Just Arabella's little sister.'

'No, you're not,' he replied gently, so gently it brought tears to her eyes.

She dashed them away with the back of her hand. 'Let me go.'

'Not yet.' His eyes rested on her face. 'You mustn't think that, Esme. I know it might seem at times that you're in her shadow...'

'In her shadow?' He really had no idea. 'I'm not even that. I'm invisible. Totally blanked out. Sometimes I wonder if I'm there at all.'

'God, no, Esme.' He brushed away the tears still falling with his fingers. 'You're more there than she's ever going to be. Kinder. Funnier. Sweeter.'

Esme recognised he was trying to make her feel better, but it didn't help. Right at this moment she didn't want to be regarded as these things. She wanted to be to him what Arabella had been. Sexy and beautiful and desirable.

'If I'm so bloody wonderful,' she cried back, 'why don't you ever ask *me* out?'

'I…you…' He was clearly taken aback by the very idea of it. 'But, Esme, you're too young. You must understand that?'

She didn't; nor did she try. She was old enough for this, old enough to feel the knot in her throat and the kick in her stomach just because he was near.

'You're such a coward!' she accused, love not precluding anger. 'You can't just say: I don't fancy you, Esme. You're not good-looking enough or smart enough.'

'But I don't think that,' he insisted.

'Then kiss me!' The words flew out of her mouth before she could stop them, but it was what she wanted.

'Esme.' His tone turned to warning. 'Look, if this is some kind of game, it's a rather dangerous one to play with men, whether you're experienced or not.'

'Oh, forget it!' His reluctance was a slap in the face. She didn't want a lecture to boot. Hurt and humiliated, she retaliated with the nastiest thing she could think of. 'You're not a man, anyway. No wonder Arabella dumped you.'

He swore for the first time. 'You really are asking for it.'

Esme felt the hands on her bare arms begin to bruise her flesh. She wasn't scared but exhilarated.

'Go on, then.'

'Fine!'

It was both expected and unexpected, a mixture of threat and lesson as he dragged her body closer and covered her mouth with his.

There was nothing loving or soft about the kiss. Lips pressed hard on hers, tongue pushed against teeth, forcing entry. She would have pulled away but a hand was suddenly in her hair, dragging her head back, keeping her there while his mouth moved on hers, tasting, invading, giving her life and breath until she moaned in unconscious pleasure.

She'd never been kissed like that before. It was a revelation. Shocked rigid one moment, then bones fluid the next, grasping for a lifeline, his shoulders, neck, wanting to touch as he was now touching her, a hand on her breast, cupping its fullness through her dress, rubbing against a nipple, found pert and hard despite her clothing.

It was Jack who finally pulled away, but only to rest his forehead against hers while they both panted for breath.

'See what I mean?' he said when he could finally talk.

'No.' She refused to see.

'Another man might not stop here,' he added, muffled as his lips tasted the damp skin at her temple.

'Then don't. Teach me a lesson!' she almost taunted in return.

'*Esme…*' Her name was a groan of protest, lost as, boldened by whisky and love, she sought his mouth once more.

Control went quickly, drowned by need, as they kissed and touched and learnt each other's bodies. Shy and reluctant with others, Esme felt nothing but overwhelming desire for this man. It was as if she had been born for him, waiting all her life to do this.

When he spread the blanket on the hard boards beneath them, she sank with him onto the makeshift bed.

They kissed again, then he murmured against her mouth, 'Are you covered?'

'Covered?'

'The Pill.'

The barest hesitation, before murmuring back, 'Yes,' understanding he would stop otherwise.

Then, legs entwined, bodies straining, he shifted her on her side and she helped him as he tugged off her now ruined dress and unbuttoned his own shirt. Cold earlier, she was now on fire, his naked flesh burning against hers.

He slid down the straps of the camisole she wore underneath until her breasts were exposed, full and ripe, the breasts of a woman. But the flesh was tender, never before touched by a man, and she arched back in surprise and delight as he put his mouth to them and circled the pink aureoles with his tongue until her nipples were so hard she couldn't bear it. She acted out of instinct rather than experience as she lifted her breast to his mouth, demanding that he satisfy this exquisite need.

And Jack? He was too far gone to do otherwise. His body had long since grown hard, painfully so, made worse as he sucked with teeth and lips on her swollen breasts and she arched beneath him, hips rising, pushing against his own flesh.

It was a shock to find her so willing. He'd thought her different from Arabella but she wasn't. The realisation at the edges of a brain fuzzy with alcohol stilled any last vestige of conscience over her youth.

They had gone too far to stop and Esme didn't want to, anyway. Not even when he began to touch her between her thighs and she stirred like a nervous filly about to be broken. She was lucky. He was gentle, oh, so gentle. She felt her body opening to him, let him slide a finger inside, caught her breath when he began to stroke her. Making her ready.

Then he straddled her and she discovered she was not ready enough. It hurt. Goodness, it hurt. She wanted to cry out. Bit her lip instead until the tearing sensation subsided.

He went still, too. As if he'd felt something. Had a moment's doubt.

Esme tried to conceal it. Her gift to him, but it had to be a secret. She moved. Lifting hips to close round him, a sensual invitation no man would refuse.

Jack didn't. He turned his head to kiss her once more, then raised himself and pushed again, deep inside her this time. She tensed, waiting for the pain, only it had gone. Or was overwhelmed. Suddenly there was pleasure. Different from any she had ever known. Running through blood and bone. Mounting with each thrust. Filling her. Obliterating self. Till they were one body, gasping and cleaving and coming, one soul, crying out in the darkness, lost to the world.

That was the first time they'd made love.

Remembered perfectly by Esme, ten years on.

Well, why not? It had also been the last.

She stopped herself thinking past that point, though she

recalled it well enough, too. What he'd said—a let-down. How she'd felt—crippled by it.

She understood now that she'd been too young, emotionally. She didn't blame him. Well, she did sometimes when she thought of how he'd been able to walk away while she was still living with the consequences.

Not just Harry. But other stuff. Like the fact she hadn't gone out with another man for years, hadn't gone to bed with one for even longer than that. And how it never really worked for her. As if the sexual side of her had been born and died on that one same night.

Or maybe it was just asleep. Like in a fairytale, needing the handsome prince to unlock the spell. Only in her case the handsome prince had returned to give her a dose of realism. Perhaps that would work just as well.

A good thing, maybe, that Jack had reappeared, enabling her to confront the past. As long as that was where he stayed. A quick walk-on part, then out of her life for ever.

Once again she considered the possibility of him actually buying Highfield, then shook her head over it. No. Not likely. He wasn't a sentimentalist. Highfield was needing major restoration. And, as he said, there were other places.

No problem, then.

CHAPTER FOUR

A MONTH passed and Jack Doyle failed to reappear. Esme began to relax, almost back to normal, no longer thinking of him daily. She had other concerns: Harry turning ten and even more insular, problems with work, her changing relationship with Charles.

The latter was her own doing. A few days after Jack Doyle had viewed Highfield, Harry had gone to stay overnight with a friend while she went to a dinner party with Charles and some mutual friends.

They had had an enjoyable evening and, once back at the cottage, she'd invited him in for coffee. It hadn't been the first time. Or the first time he'd tried to make their goodnight kiss more intimate. What had been different was her reaction.

Not spontaneous. Definitely not. Planned even when she'd been donning her glad rags for the party. That night, if Charles kissed her, she wouldn't do her usual turn and slide out of his arms. She would let him kiss her and kiss him back in the hope that she would feel all the right things.

So what had gone wrong?

Nothing really. He had kissed. She had shut her eyes and kissed back. Fine so far. A brief flare of passion. Better. Dying quickly. Then over.

Not the kiss. That had gone on as long as Esme considered polite, but it had been a relief when Charles had finally come up for air. Less of one when he'd smiled as if he'd just won the prize.

Hadn't he noticed? Maybe not. Maybe he was used to kissing emotionally repressed girls. Poor Charles.

Sympathy, however, only extended so far and, when he'd begun to kiss her again she'd pushed at his shoulders until he released her.

He had looked confused, unable to see why a green light had suddenly turned red on him.

Esme had felt he deserved some kind of explanation and launched into a 'not being ready for involvement' speech.

But Charles hadn't been listening. He'd been too busy apologising for 'rushing her' and promising to 'be patient,' and before Esme had been able to finish he'd been out of the door with a, 'Call you soon.'

Infused with guilt, Esme had watched him drive away. Far from killing his hopes, she'd somehow left him with the impression that it was only a matter of time. But she had known it wasn't. Had known from the start, if she was honest.

As for his rushing things, that was more sad than funny. Six months they'd been seeing each other, and all that time he'd scrupulously respected the distance she kept, believing, despite Harry's existence, that she was a *nice* girl.

She wondered now how he would feel if he ever discovered the real her—or that other her, anyway, the one who'd gone from a kiss to full, consensual sex with Jack Doyle in a relationship that had lasted all of forty minutes from start to finish.

Appalled, she imagined. She was herself. She had been within hours of the deed. Afterwards she'd blamed the demon drink.

It wasn't me, Your Lordship. It was the whisky.

Tough. I sentence you to teenage pregnancy and a lifetime of penury.

Well, hardly that. She had Great-Aunt Jemima's money, though as it was only a small annual sum, she hardly qualified as a trust-fund baby. Still, it was more than some had.

So count your blessings and be grateful.

Good old Jemima, pincher of cheeks, scorner of men, an all-round scary old lady.

Esme smiled briefly, before she became aware of what she was doing. Having conversations with herself again. Well, where was the harm? So maybe she'd turn a little batty, like her maiden aunt, but there were worse things on heaven and earth. Like dating suitable young men simply to avoid talking to oneself.

She had gone to bed that night resolved to finish with Charles, and woken in the same frame of mind. She'd tried to do it gradually, with work and childcare excuses, and had hoped Charles would take the hint, but he hadn't. When he'd finally pressed her into accepting a restaurant date, she had gone with the intention of making a clean break, only to discover that the dinner was to celebrate his birthday.

It said it all, really, that she'd forgotten. And, typically, Charles hadn't fanfared it. He was too diffident, maddeningly so. But how could she have said, *Happy Birthday,* followed by, *You're dumped*?

She couldn't have and didn't, had even let Charles kiss her again. Still no fireworks. Just guilt that she'd allowed this situation to develop.

She'd felt no better when her mother had called later the next morning to enquire, 'How was your dinner?'

'Dinner?'

'Last night with Charles. You were seen. Bibi Masterson.'

Esme sighed inwardly. Her mother seemed to have spies everywhere.

She continued relentlessly, 'Bibi wanted to know if there were wedding bells in the air or what.'

'I hope you told her *or what,*' Esme said with grim determination. 'I'm certainly tired of telling you, Mother.'

'Fine. You live your life the way you want to,' her mother said in slightly offended tones. 'I just felt I should call and tell you: I've sold the house.'

'What?' exclaimed Esme, closely followed by, 'When? Who to?'

'To whom,' her mother corrected, before answering first, 'It was finalised last Monday.'

Six days ago and she was only telling her now? Still, it was done, a *fait accompli.*

Esme accepted that, even as she persisted, 'To whom, Mother?'

'An American buyer,' her mother replied on a vague note.

'Peter Collins showed him round. He thought it best. I mean you didn't exactly do a great selling job on the house the last time.'

'That was Jack Doyle, Mother,' Esme reminded her heavily.

'So?' her mother dismissed. 'I don't care who buys Highfield. A ghastly pop star or even more ghastly footballer. They're welcome to it.'

Had her mother ever loved the house? It seemed not.

'Anyway,' she ran on, 'as far as the cottage is concerned, the new people have been made aware you're a sitting tenant and, as such, can't be evicted provided you pay your rent.'

'Rent?' Esme's voice rose with anxiety. 'But I don't pay rent!'

'Yes, I know, darling.' Her mother's tone was heavily patient. 'But if we'd admitted you were merely the daughter of the house, they could have insisted on vacant possession.'

'But won't they find out?' Esme queried.

'Eventually, perhaps,' her mother agreed, 'but meanwhile our solicitor has backdated a tenancy agreement in the name of E.S. Hamilton and no one has made the connection... Of course, you will have to pay rent to them.'

How much? Esme could have asked, but she knew her mother wouldn't have a clue.

'I've done my best for you, darling,' her mother concluded at Esme's silence, 'and a little gratitude wouldn't go amiss.'

Esme counted slowly to ten before responding, 'Thank you, Mother.'

Her mother didn't seem to notice how forced it was as she went on to what she regarded as a more important matter— Arabella and her intention of returning to England in the summer.

Esme listened with half a mind, and only when her mother rang off did she realise that she still didn't have an idea when the new owners would be moving in.

She debated whether she should go up to the house on the Saturday, as usual, to clean and dust, but, in the end did so partly to say goodbye to the house.

Harry tagged along, earning his pocket money by brushing and dusting while she cleaned windows. Halfway through she let him disappear outside to the garages, where various boxes and ramps provided an ideal practice strip for his skateboarding.

She went upstairs to tackle sinks and baths, which seemed to collect dirt even when unused. It was hardly a sentimental way of bidding farewell to Highfield and she was surprised how little she felt, perhaps because it was now such an empty shell.

She was finished and contemplating the furniture left in her old bedroom when she heard footsteps on the stairs.

Harry, she assumed, until a female voice called, 'Hello, is anyone there?'

The new owner, Esme concluded, and wished she could just disappear.

She walked out of the room to find a smart-suited woman standing on the upper gallery and felt at an immediate disadvantage in old jeans and T-shirt.

'Hi,' the woman drawled in an American accent, 'I guess you're from the cleaning company?'

Esme admitted it looked that way, with her clutching a feather duster in one hand. And, yes, she supposed that was what she was—the cleaner. At any rate, it seemed easier to accept that role.

'I didn't realise anyone was moving in today,' she responded. 'If you want me to go—'

'Hell, no!' the woman dismissed. 'From what I can see we'll need an army of you. How long since this place has been occupied?'

'Three years almost.'

The woman wrinkled her nose. 'Looks more like ten. When did they last decorate, I wonder?'

Esme could have answered that, too, but let it pass. She didn't think this woman would appreciate hearing it was more than a decade ago.

'Still, it has possibilities.' The woman was speaking more

to herself this time. 'Although personally I prefer my houses new and draughtproof.'

Esme was confused and a little rankled. 'You must have liked something about Highfield to have bought it.'

'Heavens, no, *I* haven't bought it!' the woman denied with a laugh. 'It's J.D.'s baby. He's downstairs, checking the place out.'

Esme's heart went into freefall: J.D.? As in…?

No, she told herself. Ridiculous. Why should it be? There were lots of people with those initials and this woman was American, so wouldn't J.D. be, too? An American buyer, that was what her mother had said.

'Hold on while I holler—' The woman leaned over the banister '—J.D., it's all right. Up here. Someone from the cleaning company.'

It drew no response.

'We thought it might be burglars,' she continued to Esme, 'because the alarm wasn't activated. I assume you switched it off.'

Esme nodded mutely. She considered explaining who she really was, then remembered she couldn't be daughter of the house *and* tenant of the cottage. So she just stood, staring silently at the other woman, conscious that she must be giving a good impression of being as vacant as the house.

'I'll go down,' the American finally added. 'He's obviously not heard me. I'll leave you to get on.'

'Yes, fine.' Esme watched the other woman descend the staircase, wondering what she should do.

Instinct told her to pack up quickly and leave rather than stick around to discover the identity of J.D. The problem was she couldn't see a way of getting out of the house without encountering someone. And there was Harry.

The thought of him sent her back inside her bedroom and over to the window. He was still in the courtyard, practising turns on his board. No sign of anyone else. She considered tapping on the glass but that might bring him inside. What to do?

She was still deliberating when she heard footsteps ascending the stairs. The man? Probably. She looked round the room for somewhere to hide, then told herself to stop being ridiculous. What were the chances of it being Jack? And even if it was, how pathetic to hide from him!

So she stood there, listening to footsteps echoing on bare boards as they approached her door, the only one open.

The surprised, 'You!' came from the man as he entered, not Esme, dreading yet half expecting Jack Doyle, expensively casual in chino trousers and designer polo shirt.

'Me,' she agreed simply.

He frowned, glanced at the feather duster in her hand, the brush leaning against one wall and back to her, dressed in knee-ripped jeans and smeared T-shirt with her long blonde hair caught up in a pony-tail.

'I thought you were joking,' he said at length, 'about *doing* people's houses.'

She had been. This was the only house she *did* in that sense.

But a devil inside made her say, 'We all have to make a living.'

'True,' he conceded, 'but it's hard to reconcile—you a cleaner.'

'It's called social mobility,' shrugged Esme. 'Some people go up in the world and some down. I'm not your cleaning company, by the way. Your friend misunderstood.'

'I know.' He nodded. 'They aren't due till Monday... What are you doing here exactly?'

Esme would have thought it obvious, so couldn't resist a dry, 'You'll need a domestic. What better way to interview for the post?'

He smiled quizzically. 'Are you serious?'

'My life's ambition—' this time the sarcasm in her voice couldn't be missed '—to grow up, lose my family home to the cook's son, then be reincarnated as his Mrs Mop.'

She didn't care if the 'cook's son' comment epitomised snobbery. She had to have some weapons against him.

He pulled a face, recognising irony. 'It did seem unlikely, your condescending to work for me. Though I can't imagine it's much different cleaning for "nobs"—or do they generate a better class of dirt?'

Esme supposed she'd asked for that and confined herself to pulling a face back at him.

'So what does *Mr* Mop do?' he resumed more casually, shoving his hands in his pockets as he strolled towards a window.

'*Mr Mop?* What makes you think there is one?' Esme tried to distract him from looking out.

Already too late as he nodded towards the courtyard below. 'That is *Master* Mop down there, isn't it? Your son, from the look of him.'

Esme followed his gaze. Harry was now sitting on the step used for mounting horses, his face in profile as he read a book.

She told herself not to panic. He'd seen Harry's likeness to her and no one else.

'Yes, he's mine,' she admitted briefly.

'And Mr Mop?'

'Long gone and forgotten.'

'Right.' It was a non-judgemental comment.

But Esme still felt judged. Like most single mothers. Irrelevant that they didn't volunteer for the role.

'He's pretty good on the board,' Jack added almost conversationally. 'I was watching earlier before I realised he was yours. How old is he?'

Esme was ahead, anticipating the question, lying seamlessly, 'Nine.'

He raised a brow. 'He looks tall for his age?'

'Yes, he is, *very*,' she laboured. Harry was also tall for his real age of ten.

'What's his name?'

'Harry…Harry *Hamilton.*'

Esme stressed the surname, obliquely claiming Harry as all her own. It didn't stop Jack Doyle, however.

'So who was his father,' he enquired, 'if you don't mind me asking?'

Esme was a past master at avoiding this question. 'I do, actually.'

The trouble with Jack Doyle, was that he wasn't like other people. If he noticed a hint, he ignored it.

'One of the Fairfaxes,' he mused aloud, 'what was his name? The youngest brother who used to moon around after you at riding events?'

'Henry,' she supplied without thinking.

'That's the one,' he confirmed. 'Henry...interesting. Isn't that the name from which Harry is derived?'

'It is also the name of my grandfather,' Esme responded heavily.

'So, should I take that as a denial?'

About to nod, Esme stopped herself. Did it matter if she left him with the impression Harry was Henry Fairfax's? It was years since she'd seen Henry but she knew he lived somewhere abroad—South Africa, or South America, perhaps. Too far away, at any rate, for there to be any comeback.

'I'd take it as a mind-your-own-business,' she replied at length.

He laughed briefly. 'Ambiguous.'

Well, that was what Esme was aiming for. Time to leave, she decided.

She made a show of looking at her watch. 'I have to go.'

'Lunch date?' he enquired.

Esme didn't answer. He'd already asked too many questions for her liking.

'I thought *I* might take you somewhere,' he added as she made to walk away. 'The Sherborne Hotel in Addleston, assuming it still exists.'

Esme gaped at him. 'Why?'

'*Why?*' he echoed. 'Do I need a reason?'

'Yes.'

'Well, let's see... It might be interesting to get to know each other again.'

Esme continued to stare at him. Why should he suddenly want to know her now?

'I can't think what else there is to know,' she responded

at length. 'You're Jack Doyle, internet entrepreneur and new owner of Highfield. I'm Esme Hamilton, single mother of one and ex-cleaner of your mansion. Do you think we have any common ground?'

The final was a parting shot, as she raised an eyebrow at him before heading for the door.

But if she'd imagined he'd just let her walk away, she was mistaken. He caught up with her on the galleried landing, a hand on her elbow forcing her to stop and turn.

'Is it Highfield?' he asked bluntly. 'Is that the problem? You can't bear for me, the cook's son, to have it?'

Esme's eyes widened at the slant he'd put on things. The animosity she felt was unconnected to house deeds and family origins.

'It couldn't just be you, could it?' she flashed back, trying and failing to free her arm. 'That I don't want to have lunch with you because you're too damn boring for words or too bigheaded to take no for a bloody answer!'

She didn't have to feign anger. She *was* angry. With him. With herself. With the whole world, for that matter.

He took a step back from her, perhaps recalling how she'd slapped him at their last reunion, but he didn't release her arm. Nor did he show any sign of having his ego deflated.

'I guess that's telling it like it is,' he finally drawled back, 'although a little tip for the future: if you really don't like a man, it's best not to make those little moaning sounds when he's kissing you. Might give him the whole wrong idea.'

He was talking of their last meeting and Esme felt her face burn even as temper prompted denial. 'I did not!'

'Didn't you, now?' he challenged. 'I think maybe a rerun is in order.'

'Wh-what do you mean?' Could one fear something and long for it in the same instant?

It seemed so as he lived up to the threat and pulled her into his arms, silencing protest with his warm, hard lips.

Part of her resisted, issuing a muffled curse, pushing at his broad shoulders, as she struggled to be free of the embrace. But the other part? It was gasping for sanity as she opened her mouth and took the breath from his and let him taste her with his tongue, and felt the treacherous sensation curling in the belly pressed against his hard flesh.

She was fighting herself, balling her fingers into fists so she wouldn't touch him back, catching the sounds in her throat even as she strained for his kiss, dizzy with desire when he finally let her go and having to grip onto the banister to stop herself swaying.

His own chest heaving, Jack stared hard at her as he tried to figure out the mixed messages he was receiving. He knew his own feelings. He wanted her more than he had any woman in a long time. Meant to have her, too, despite—or maybe because of—the furious resentment in her eyes.

'How serious is it with you and this other fellow?'

'Other fellow?'

Esme's mind had gone blank.

'The one you were waiting for at the West Gate.'

That one.

'Oh, you mean…' she scanned her fuddled brain for a name '…Charles.'

'Charles?' He mocked her posh accent. 'Landed gentry, is he?'

'Yes, actually.'

'And is it?'

'What?'

'Serious?'

'Yes!'

She lied without conscience.

'But scarcely satisfying?'

'What?'

This 'what' came from disbelief.

He continued regardless.

'Well, at the risk of being called bigheaded a second time—' his tone was dry '—I don't think you'd be respond-ing to me if everything was OK between you and Charles.'

'I wasn't!' Esme refuted automatically.

'Really?' He arched a brow. 'In that case, I can't wait to

find out what it's like when you do respond... Though, on second thoughts, I just about remember.'

His mouth moved into a slow smile as he alluded to their long-ago tryst.

Esme remembered, too. All of it. That was why she wasn't going down that road again.

'Won't your girlfriend mind?' She hadn't forgotten the woman downstairs, even if he had.

'Rebecca?' He followed her glance to the hall below. 'I wouldn't think so, considering she's married to my partner.'

'Oh.'

'I'm currently unattached,' he added.

'Well, I'm not!' Esme claimed, and, wondering why she was even having this ridiculous conversation, ended it by walking away.

This time he didn't stop her but followed on behind as she descended the sweeping staircase.

Esme fought a desire to break into a run, and, with him still on her heels when she reached the kitchen, was relieved to find the woman, Rebecca, there.

'I've made coffee,' the American woman directed at Jack, then at Esme, 'Would you like some, too?'

'No, thanks,' she replied. 'I've finished for the day.'

'R-right.' The older woman looked doubtful. 'But you are coming back? This place is going to need some radical work before you can live in it, J.D., and not just cleaning. Now I know why you English call these places stately piles.'

Her outspokenness was tempered by a grin and, out of the corner of her eye, Esme caught Jack grinning back.

'Possibly,' he agreed, 'but, before you say more, I'd better perform some introductions. Esme Scott-Hamilton, meet Rebecca Wiseman. Rebecca, this is Esme, daughter of the former owner.'

'Oops,' came from Rebecca, 'someone take my foot out of my mouth, will you?'

She pulled a face of apology and offered Esme her hand. Esme shook it briefly, muttering, 'Pleased to meet you.'

'Likewise,' Rebecca returned. 'Sorry about earlier, thinking you were the cleaner. Why didn't you say something?'

'I am the cleaner,' Esme claimed unashamedly.

Wrongfooted again, Rebecca replied, 'I think I'll just shut up now.'

'Don't worry about it,' Jack told her. 'Esme isn't that sensitive, are you?'

Wasn't she? Clearly not in his view, anyway. Otherwise why did he continuously ride roughshod over her feelings?

'I wouldn't have to be.' The dig was directed at him rather than Rebecca, before she was distracted by the sight of Harry approaching the back door.

He stopped short of coming inside but he gave her an I'm-bored-can-we-go look which mobilised her to pick up the denim jacket she'd slung over the back of a kitchen chair.

'Is that your brother? He's one heck of a handsome boy,' declared Rebecca in warm tones.

As a mother, Esme appreciated hearing nice things about her child and smiled back, 'Thanks, but he's actually my son.'

'*Your son?*' Rebecca didn't have to feign incredulity. 'Amazing, you look far too young!'

'Thanks,' Esme murmured again at the intended compliment.

It was Jack who muttered, 'She probably was.'

Esme didn't know whether he was trying to be funny or insulting but it took all her control not to snap back, *It didn't stop you!*

'*Jack!*' Rebecca reproved before telling Esme, 'Never mind him. He's so scared of commitment he'll be seventy before he gets married, far less has children.'

'Not true,' Jack denied, mouth slanting, 'I've just been waiting for the right woman to come along.'

Grey eyes came to rest on Esme and stayed there.

She could have flattered herself but she'd ceased being a fool the day she'd become a mother. Too young, maybe, but, as a means of wising up, nothing could beat it.

They traded stares, Jack's mocking, Esme's merely hostile.

It was Rebecca who laughed, 'Talk about corny lines,' while the other two continued their staring competition until Esme finally threw in the towel.

'I have to go,' she announced, breaking off eye contact and heading for the door.

She knew he wouldn't stop her in front of his friend but she hadn't counted on him pursuing her outside to the court-yard, where Harry was again seated on the mounting block.

Her son's face brightened as he saw her before registering the man with a curious look.

'Why are you following me?' she hissed at Jack.

'I'd like to meet your boy,' he replied simply.

Esme resisted asking why and concentrated on keeping her cool.

'Well, don't expect him to be sociable.' She knew Harry could be aloof with strangers.

'Like his mother, then,' Jack said under his breath before coolly introducing himself to Harry. 'Hi, I'm Jack Doyle, an old friend of your mother's.'

Friend? Esme almost snorted aloud and waited for Harry's usual mumble.

'That's weird!' he responded instead. 'I'm reading your book.'

'You write books?' Esme's tone was accusing.

The man was more amused. 'Not guilty.'

Harry chipped in, '*This* book, Mum. The one I'm reading. It's got his name in the front.'

'Oh, right.' Esme belatedly remembered Harry unearthing a box of old books behind a hatch in his bedroom and wondered how she was going to explain this coincidence.

Jack read the title from the spine of the book. '*The Time Machine* by H.G. Wells. That's pretty advanced reading for your age.'

Harry gave a modest shrug. 'The story's quite good when you get into it, as long as you ignore his theories of time and space travel. They're a bit crazy.'

Jack raised a brow in Esme's direction, impressed by her

son's intelligence, before referring to the book again. 'Where did you find it?'

'A charity shop,' Esme put in quickly, only to have Harry contradict her.

'No, it wasn't,' he denied. 'It was in our house, in a box behind a hatch in the attic.'

'Your house?' Jack slid a quizzical glance at Esme. 'Where do you live exactly?'

Esme started to say, 'South—' the name of the local town. But, quicker off the mark, Harry stated, 'The cottage in the grounds.'

'Really?' Dark brows were raised as Jack concluded for himself, 'So you're the sitting tenant?'

'Yes.' At least he hadn't said "my" sitting tenant, but Esme suspected him of inward gloating.

Harry was oblivious of undercurrents. 'Are you the new owner?'

Jack nodded.

'Cool,' was Harry's verdict.

Jack smiled.

By now Esme was gritting her teeth so hard she might have done damage to them.

'How long have you lived there?' asked Jack.

'About eight years,' she responded flatly.

'Even when your mother was still occupying the main house?' He frowned.

Esme gave a nod and thought to add, 'We rented it from her.'

'A peppercorn rent, presumably?' he commented.

How to answer that? Have her mother seem meaner than she actually was or jeopardise her position as sitting tenant?

'What's peppercorn mean?' Harry put in.

'I'll tell you later,' answered Esme, making another show of looking at her watch. 'Is that the time? We have to go... Here, you'll be needing these.'

She handed over the bunch of keys weighing down her coat pocket and finally took to her heels, leaving Harry to follow.

She heard Jack say, 'Nice to meet you, Harry.'

'You, too,' Harry replied, slow to trail after her.

She waited at the end of the stable block until he caught up. A backward glance and she saw the man still watching after them, meeting her gaze with a slanting smile.

'See you around,' he called out.

Only the boy answered, 'See you,' before being hurried down the path through the woods.

Jack continued to gaze after them. It was quite a turn-up, Esme now living in the cottage. He wondered why she'd kept quiet about it. Worried about her tenancy status, perhaps?

'Taking a walk down memory lane?' Rebecca asked as she appeared at his side.

Jack had told her about his past associations with the estate. 'Not really. The place has changed too much.'

'And the girl?' Rebecca smiled.

'Especially the girl.' Jack still couldn't quite reconcile the new Esme with the old. Tall, slim and blonde, she was undoubtedly better looking than the cute, slightly dumpy kid that had used to follow him around. But at what cost?

His speculative air fed Rebecca's curiosity. 'So, how well did you know her? A victim of the undoubted Jack Doyle charm, or shouldn't I ask?'

Jack shook his head. He could have told her the truth; Rebecca and her husband Sam were his closest friends. But it didn't seem right to confess his one-time thing with Esme, even if he'd been one in a line and she'd gone on, soon after, to have that boy. For a moment he'd actually wondered if he could be...but no, the age was wrong.

'Miss Esme?' he said, tongue-in-cheek. 'Too elevated for the likes of me, I'm afraid.'

Rebecca laughed, as intended. 'Not now, though, Mr Moneybags.'

Jack made a slight face. 'Somehow I don't think that'll impress her.'

'And we want to do that, do we?' Rebecca teased back.

'Perhaps,' Jack agreed, although he kept to himself the way he really felt.

Walking back to the cottage, Esme tried to do the same, but Harry wasn't fooled.

'What's wrong?' He'd rarely seen his mother so impatient.

'Nothing!' she claimed, while keeping up this pace all the way to her door.

Once inside, Harry pursued, 'Is it that man? Don't you like him?'

Like, or dislike, for that matter, didn't come at all close to the feeling she had for Jack Doyle—a powerful cocktail of fear, anger and sexual chemistry.

'Not much,' she stated at length.

'Because he bought the house?' Harry reasoned.

'Partly.' Easiest to agree.

Ever logical, Harry pointed out, 'Someone had to buy it.'

'Yes, well, I'd have preferred it was someone else,' she returned. 'Now, can we just change the subject?'

Nettled, Harry took her literally and flatly informed her, 'You have a cobweb in your hair,' before heading for his room.

'Ugh!' Esme put a hand to her head and patted round it until she found the offending object. She brushed it out with her fingers and shook her head.

What must she have looked like? Old jeans, baggy shirt, hair in a pony-tail and none too clean. A complete contrast to the elegance of his American woman friend. Yet he'd kissed her.

So? she demanded of herself. Was that meant to be a consolation?

No, more an indication that Jack Doyle hadn't changed. He was still an opportunist. Willing to take what was on offer, regardless.

Only she wasn't. On offer, that was. And the sooner he realised it the better.

The trouble was he still thought of her as Midge, needy younger sister to the more attractive Arabella. Or was his abiding memory of her the girl in the hayloft who'd proved so very easy?

She let her mind wander back once more to the night Harry

had been conceived and this time forced herself to remember the rest...

They lay for a moment or two, catching breath, recovering sanity.

Then he murmured, 'God, that was good.'

Briefly gratified, Esme let the words sink in. Good as in marks out of ten. Not good as in this has made me love you.

A silly dream, worthy of a silly schoolgirl.

'Are you OK?' He stroked the hair back from her face.

'Yes, fine.' Don't cry. Mustn't cry. After all, she'd volunteered for this. Begged for it, some might say. How could she have known it would leave her feeling this empty?

'I just thought for a minute there...' He hesitated, reluctant to voice his concern. 'Well, that I might have hurt you.'

Asking without asking: were you a virgin?

Esme wondered what he'd say if she told him the truth.

She shook her head instead and detached herself from feeling. 'No, I'm just cold.'

She shivered for effect, then found herself shivering for real.

He hugged her against his chest, his body hair warm against her bare skin, but she trembled all the more.

It was then he sat away from her, feeling for the torch and their clothes.

'Here.' He found her dress, and, not bothering with underwear, pulled it over her head.

She behaved like a robotic doll, raising her arms to slip into the sleeveless garment, lowering them as he zipped it up at the back.

She heard him rustle into his own shirt, the only piece of clothing he'd fully taken off, before he picked up his denim jacket and draped it back round her shoulders.

She still felt chilled and, worse, stone-cold sober.

'Let's go somewhere warmer.' He slipped the shoes back on her feet and helped her towards the ladder, going first to guide her down each rung.

Once on solid ground, Esme wanted to flee. She made the door before he caught her arm.

'Esme?' He angled the torch so they could see each other's faces.

'Yes?' She turned and waited for words that could make this right.

'You know I never meant for this to happen—'

Not those words.

'Yes?' Defiant this time.

'I do like you,' he added. 'I like you very much.'

Just not enough, Esme added for herself.

'And who knows,' he continued softly, 'maybe one day I'll come back and we'll—?'

'Look—' Esme didn't want his empty promises '—we had sex. It's no big deal.'

She tried to sound blasé. Perhaps she managed. His voice certainly hardened.

'Well, it should be,' he told her. 'The world hasn't changed that much, and if you go in for casual sex, well... Boys talk, Esme. I'd hate you to end up with a reputation.'

Esme felt her face go redder and redder, a mixture of embarrassment and temper. How dared he have sex with her, then follow it up with a lecture?

'You hypocrite!' she spat the word at him. 'You sanctimonious bastard! You bloody—'

'You're right, I'm no better,' he admitted, cutting across her. 'Worse, even, knowing you're just a kid. And, yes, I enjoyed it. So much that, if I weren't leaving, I'd be back tomorrow night. But you're no Arabella. You're—'

'*Arabella! Arabella! Arabella!*' Esme didn't want to hear how she compared with her sister. 'You're as pathetic as I am. Do you think she gives a damn about you?' she demanded, meaning to hurt him as he was hurting her.

'That's not the point!' He held onto her arm while she tried to wrest free. 'What I'm trying to say—'

'I don't care what you're saying!' She was crying now with angry humiliation.

'Look, calm down, will you, unless you want an audience?' He glanced in warning towards the big house, where the upper floors were lit.

Esme followed his gaze, and, made aware that somebody could be watching them, swallowed hard and fought back further tears. But she had no intention of calming down. She just wanted to get away.

She went still, fooling him into believing she was acquiescent, then the moment he released her she ran.

The move caught him by surprise and she was halfway across the back yard before he called out for her to stop. She kept running, casting off his jacket as she did so.

He pursued her, something she hadn't anticipated.

As she ran towards the back door she prayed Maggie, the new cook, had left it unlocked. Luck in, she was through it and shooting the bolt seconds before Jack got there and turned the outer handle.

'Esme?' he urged from the other side.

She stayed where she was, leaning against the heavy wood, trusting he couldn't hear her laboured breathing.

'Esme?' He rattled on the handle. 'Let me in. We have to talk.'

She did not respond.

'Esme.' A hand slammed on the door in frustration.

She waited, tears streaming.

Till finally he went...

And here she was, more than ten years on, still feeling the humiliation. Not that it had been deliberately inflicted. She understood that. Nor was it the sex she minded, although that first taste of it seemed to have left her emotionally debilitated.

It was the pity he'd felt for her. That was the worst of it. As if she was a lame duck—or perhaps the proverbial ugly duckling—whom he'd briefly noticed, only to regret his interest almost instantly.

The fact that he'd come up to the house the next day to say goodbye hadn't healed any wounds. She'd been out—gone, in fact, to stay with a schoolfriend in London. He'd left a message with Maggie. No letter, as he'd claimed, but a simple, 'Tell Esme she deserves better.'

How she'd blushed when Maggie had relayed it on her return. Thankfully the cook hadn't asked for any explanation. Perhaps she'd believed it to mean that Esme deserved better than the family she had.

Esme hadn't been altogether certain of his meaning either. Better than what? Better than him? Or better than turning into the type of woman who slept around?

She'd never been that. He'd confused her with Arabella. Only, in Arabella's case, he'd been prepared to forgive promiscuity.

Because he'd loved her?

There seemed no other explanation, and even now Esme could feel pangs of jealousy. Ridiculous, really. She should have got over it long ago. She'd thought she had.

But that had been when Jack Doyle was consigned to the far, murky reaches of her memory, reduced in size, importance and physical attraction. That was before he'd come breezing back into her life, better looking than ever in his thirties, successful and wealthy enough to be deemed eligible by anyone's standards, so confident about his place in the world she had an urge to drag him down.

And any scruples where she was concerned? Clearly gone out of the window. After all, she was twenty-six, old enough to know better, already with a messed-up life, an unmarried mother with few prospects. He probably reckoned she would be grateful for his lunch offers—and any other offer that might proceed from it.

Well, he was wrong. The outside world might view her as a failure but she had more self-respect than she had ever had as a girl. She was bringing up a son virtually single-handed, slowly establishing a business and making her own way in the world. If she was sometimes lonely, well, surely she was strong enough to survive that rather than risk some meaningless relationship which would upset her well-ordered existence?

Let him move into the big house and play lord of the

manor, but he wouldn't be claiming anything from her apart from rent.

And Harry? That hurdle had been crossed. Jack Doyle had looked at him and failed to recognise his blood. No reason to imagine that would change—and she would never tell him.

Why should she, other than to relish his horrified reaction? And she wouldn't do that to Harry.

He deserved better, too.

CHAPTER FIVE

WORK on the estate began the very next week. On the Monday, when she accompanied Harry to the West Gate, there were already builders' vans, a mini-crane, digger and site caravan parked both outside and inside the estate.

She told herself it was no business of hers but, after Harry had climbed on board the bus, she went over to the man in charge and asked what was happening.

'Gates have to come down,' he informed her laconically.

It was just as Esme had feared. The desecration had started.

'They seem perfectly good gates to me.' She glanced towards the magnificent structures of wrought-ironwork.

'Rusted,' the man told her, 'possibly dangerous.'

'Nonsense,' she dismissed, purposely blind to the scarred paintwork and corroded hinges. 'They've been here about ninety years.'

'Old, then.' The man obviously thought she'd proved his point. 'Better talk to your husband. His orders.'

'He's not my husband!' Esme refuted immediately.

The man raised a slight brow before shrugging indifferently. 'Whatever, love, he's the boss.'

Esme could have declared who she was, but being a tenant wasn't going to cut any ice. Why should it?

She walked away instead, wishing she'd never instigated the conversation. Nothing she said or did was going to make a difference.

Jack Doyle could do what he liked to Highfield. Paint the outside pink or rip out the windows to put in aluminium double glazing. Who was to prevent him?

Not her, certainly. After their last encounter she'd decided to give Jack as wide a berth as possible until she could find somewhere else to live. Forget her rights as a sitting tenant.

She didn't think rights would stop Jack if he wanted her out and she wasn't going to wait around until he made his move.

With Harry off to school, she scoured the accommodation ads in the local papers and soon discovered that houses were outside her budget. It would have to be a flat. She called two numbers—at one there was no answer, at the other the flat had already gone.

Next she consulted the Yellow Pages for the names of letting agencies and found a couple in Southbury. She copied down addresses, having decided to visit in person. She locked up the cottage and got into her car, a cheap runaround that had seen better days.

She drove to the back gates. Or where the gates had been. Now there was just a gaping hole.

A couple of the workmen waved her through and she nodded a thank-you. It wasn't their fault, after all.

By the time she reached town she'd talked herself into a more positive frame of mind. It was time she and Harry moved on, said goodbye to their old life, started anew.

Her optimism dwindled, however, as she signed onto the books of the first agency. Had a child? Mmm, that might be a problem. She was self-employed? Could she produce accounts for the last year, then? Possibly. A reference from her current landlord as well? Difficult. Difficult to explain, too.

At least she was more clued up for the second agency. Ready for the questions and ready to say, 'Yes,' and worry later about how to conjure up non-existent accounts and reference letters. Still nothing, however, in her price bracket. Next week, perhaps. Leave her telephone number.

So she trawled back home, deflated, and tried to concentrate on her sole commission, the master bedroom for Mr and Mrs City Analysts.

By the time she went to collect Harry, a small crane was being used to position a new gate in place. She did a double take, it looked so similar to the old ones.

'Like it?' the man in charge called out as she passed.

'It's all right,' she conceded grudgingly.

'Should be,' he ran on. 'Specially commissioned. Best wrought-iron manufacturer in the country.'

'Really?'

'Wouldn't like to say how much they cost.'

Esme suspected he would. 'Will you be finished tonight?'

'No chance.' He shook his head. 'But don't worry. We'll leave the plant blocking the entrance.'

Plant? Esme almost asked, then realised he meant the machinery, crane and diggers and such.

He nodded towards the caravan. 'And one of us will be stopping, as we agreed with your man.'

She frowned, then bristled. 'If you mean Jack Doyle, the owner, he's not my man. There's a cottage in the grounds of which I am the tenant. That's all.'

'Sorry, I'm sure.' He didn't look it, smiling a little. 'Just thought: you and him... Well, natural enough.'

Esme wanted to say there was nothing natural about it, apart from the fact Jack Doyle was a man and she was a woman, but she coloured instead, remembering their last encounter.

'I hardly know the man,' she said at length before walking off.

True, in a way. She'd known the old Jack Doyle. Clever, kind, funny. The new one was a stranger. Still clever, but not so kind, and nothing funny about him being here.

With some relief she saw the school bus appear on the horizon. Harry was the only one to get off but she heard some other boys jeering at him before the doors closed.

'What's that about?' she asked as one boy thumped on the bus window as it drew past.

Harry shrugged. 'Nothing.'

It didn't seem like nothing and Esme stared after the bus with a furrowed brow.

Harry had lost interest, however, watching the workmen as they continued to position the new gate.

'I don't know why they bothered,' Esme volunteered, 'it looks almost the same as the others, give or take a spot of rust.'

'They're automatic,' Harry pointed out, 'remote control, I bet.'

'How do you know that?' his mother asked doubtfully.

'They're laying cabling.' Harry indicated the work going on on the far side, partially shielded by a van.

Esme finally noticed the trench already half-dug, leading away from the gate, ready to tap into the nearest electricity supply.

'Oh, great,' she muttered, clearly meaning the opposite, as she turned back up the road to the cottage.

'It is really,' Harry argued alongside her. 'You always said they were heavy and awkward, and now you'll be able to open them with just the touch of a button.'

'If I had a button, yes,' she replied drily.

Harry caught on. 'The new man—he's bound to give you a handset to operate them.'

Oh, bound to, would have been Esme's sarcastic response, only she kept it to herself. Being just the two of them, it was sometimes tempting to confide her worries to Harry, but it wasn't right. He was only ten.

'You wouldn't be able to drive your car out otherwise.' Harry voiced her worries aloud.

'True.' She painted a smile on her face and seized the opportunity to suggest, 'Well, we could always move, couldn't we?'

Unfortunately it went down like a lead balloon with Harry. 'Move? Move where?'

He'd obviously never considered the possibility.

'Oh, I don't know.' She was intentionally upbeat. 'Somewhere in Southbury. It would be less isolated.'

Harry pulled a face and declared unequivocally, 'I'm happy here.'

'But you might be even happier in town,' Esme ploughed on. 'You must feel lonely at times, with just me for company.'

'No,' he claimed stubbornly.

Esme held in a sigh and decided to leave things there. At least she had planted the idea of moving in his head, and by the time she found somewhere suitable he might have grown used to it.

It took two days for the West Gate to be completed, and almost immediately the construction gang moved on to re-constructing the rear driveway. Even Esme couldn't maintain it didn't need work. She had too often cursed the potholes and vegetation growing in its centre that made ominous noises as it scraped against her exhaust pipe.

She couldn't complain about the gates either, as Colin Jones, the head builder, made a point of visiting her cottage to present her with her very own remote control. Apparently Mr Doyle had instructed him to do so when he'd called from America to check their progress.

Esme just stopped herself saying, *He didn't tell me he was going away again.*

Fortunately she recognised her own absurdity. Why should Jack Doyle inform her of his movements? She was nothing to him.

And he was nothing to her, she reminded herself quickly.

But knowing he was not in residence had Esme giving way to curiosity and taking the path to the main house to see what changes were being made there.

She had expected some but was shocked to find almost every inch of the back covered in scaffolding, as the stone-work was cleaned and repaired, while the stable block was now entirely roofless in preparation for conversion into guest cottages. It seemed as if an army of workmen was there.

Unchallenged, she slipped through the open gateway at the side of the house to find a similar story at the front. Logically she recognised that Highfield needed this work to survive, but emotionally it was like watching her past being erased, leaving her rudderless.

From that point her resolve to leave the cottage became an imperative. It wasn't Jack Doyle or his alterations but a real-isation that her life had to move on. She scoured the classified ads and phoned the agencies on almost a daily basis. Harry was often a silent but, she assumed, accepting witness.

A week slipped into two, then three, before she found somewhere vaguely acceptable. She'd already viewed several so-called 'apartments' that were no better than bedsits, so when she saw the flat above the Chinese takeaway her expectations were already considerably lowered. Drawbacks like a dirty kitchen, no shower and a living room barely big enough to swing a cat in had ceased to matter. It was within her budget and seemed a veritable palace.

So much so that she talked herself into believing it was *the* place and, putting fifty pounds' deposit down, presented it to Harry.

But Harry hadn't been round dingier, filthier, more cramped possibilities and saw the place for what it was. A dump!

When Esme asked on the car journey home, 'What do you think?' Harry had no idea how much time she'd invested into finding it.

He was honest. 'It's horrible.'

For once Esme didn't appreciate Harry's straightforwardness or consider his feelings or remember, for all his intelligence, he was just a child.

She let all her anxiety out, telling him bluntly that he'd have to like it because if he imagined they could go on living in the cottage, he could think again. The cottage wasn't the family's any more. It was Jack Doyle's and sooner or later he would want it back. For his housekeeper or a friend or simply because he didn't want a couple of strangers living on his estate.

Esme gave him a dose of reality as she saw it. Unforgivable, when she'd spent the first ten years of his life shielding him from the very same reality, but she couldn't help herself. It all came tumbling out, a catalogue of money worries and insecurities, while Harry retreated into silence.

His very reserve seemed to incite her more, and only when they reached home and he disappeared to his room did she ask herself why she was telling him all this. He might be smart but he had only just turned ten, and was hardly re-

sponsible for the fact she'd messed up her life, and his along
with it.

She tried later to make up for her outburst, but he remained
solemn and largely silent, a mood that persisted over the
weekend.

Hardly the first time Esme had doubted herself as a mother
but that didn't make it any easier. It simply confirmed what
the rest of the world thought—what Jack Doyle had actually
said—that she'd been too young when she'd had Harry.

It was three days later when Harry suddenly announced, 'I
think we'll be able to stay here, Mum.'

'Oh, Harry, I want you to stop worrying about such
things,' she responded guiltily. 'I shouldn't have said what I
did, and whatever happens I'm sure everything will work out
for the best.'

'But if we could stay in the cottage forever,' he persisted,
'that's what you'd want?'

Esme didn't know how to answer that. A fresh start somewhere far from Highfield had begun to seem an attractive
option, but she appreciated Harry's reluctance to be uprooted.

'I don't know any more,' she answered honestly.

'But if Jack *wants* you to stay—' he pursued.

'Jack?' she questioned her son's familiarity with the name.
'Mr Doyle, you mean?'

Harry nodded. 'He said I should call him Jack.'

'When?' Esme didn't recall such an exchange.

Harry shrugged evasively. 'I can't remember. Does it matter? Mum, if he doesn't want us to go, then we can just stay
here, can't we?'

Esme didn't see it as that simple, but she wasn't up to any
deeper discussion with ten minutes to go to the school bus.

'It's possible,' she replied.

Her tone was noncommittal but Harry read more into it,
and his face brightened.

Coward that she was, Esme decided to leave him with this
false hope until she could present him with an alternative to
the des res above the takeaway.

But she still hadn't found anywhere when Jack Doyle reappeared at the weekend.

It was late on the Friday evening. Harry was at a birthday sleepover with his one good friend and Esme was newly out of the bath and drying her hair before the fire when the knock came.

Quiet as it was, it startled her. She never had visitors—none that didn't telephone first at least.

She crept through the hall to her downstairs bedroom and, leaving it in darkness, peeped through a curtain. It was raining outside, and almost chilly for late June, but enough light remained to recognise her caller.

Relief quickly gave way to that stomach-churning feeling she tended to get round Jack Doyle.

She dropped the curtain back in place and considered pretending she was out. She was hardly dressed for callers, although modestly enough covered by one of her mother's voluminous silk robes over her nightown.

He knocked again. 'Esme, it's Jack.'

Was that meant as reassurance?

She made no move towards the door. Perhaps he would just go away if she ignored him.

He added, 'I know you're in there, Es.'

Es. He was the only one who shortened her name like that. Once she had liked it. Now it just caused resentment.

Which was why she stopped cowering and, the next time he knocked, strode to the door, yanked it open and demanded, 'Yes?'

'Hi,' he greeted in return. 'Nice to see you, too.'

She grimaced at the sarcasm. 'What do you want? It's past nine.'

'Sorry,' he apologised with a shrug, 'but I just got back from the States.'

Esme stopped herself saying, So? Was she meant to be impressed?

'I thought I'd better come down,' he ran on, 'in case I missed you in the morning.'

'If it's about the rent,' Esme muttered back, 'I'd have paid it by now but we haven't agreed how much.'

'The rent?' he echoed, as though he hadn't given it any thought. 'I don't know. What were you paying your mother?'

Nothing. But she couldn't say that.

'A hundred and fifty pounds.' The figure came off the top of her head.

He accepted it with a nod. 'Fine.'

'A month,' she qualified quickly.

He nodded again. He was clearly indifferent to what sum she paid. Her rent was a drop in the ocean as far as his finances were concerned.

'It was actually your tenancy I wanted to discuss,' he stated evenly.

'Right.' Esme's mouth formed a tight line. Eviction time?

'If we could go inside?' He came a step closer.

Esme went into automatic retreat. Short of closing the door in his face, she had no choice.

She led the way into the living room. She tightened her robe, conscious of not being properly dressed.

He was over-dressed, if anything. Businesslike in suit and tie, although the tie was pulled down and the top button of his shirt was open.

'Would you like a drink?' The offer was grudging rather than gracious as she found herself playing reluctant hostess.

'I'd appreciate it.' He gazed around him at the changes wrought to his old home. 'It's not how I remembered it at all.'

An accusation? Maybe not. More a statement.

'The staircase is new,' she admitted. 'I had it built so Harry could use the attic as a bedroom. I changed the walls, too, taking them back to their original stone where I could, and painted the rest. Some of the furniture is your old stuff; the rest I bought at auction.'

'It's quite a transformation.' He seemed genuinely admiring. 'Hard to believe the difference in the place.'

She accepted the compliment with a brief, 'Thanks,' before asking, 'Tea, coffee, or something stronger?'

He surprised her by saying, 'Tea, I think.'

She'd expected him to ask for a whisky.

'Take a seat.' She indicated the sofa, and went through to the kitchen.

The kettle was recently boiled. She made the tea quickly as she heard him prowling round her living room. When she came through with the tray of cups and teapot he was standing by her work table in one corner, perusing sketches she had left out.

'These look professional,' he commented.

'They're for a client's bed-and dressing-rooms,' she relayed. 'Plan number ninety-nine or thereabouts.'

He absorbed this information and concluded with a slight smile, 'So that's what you meant by "Doing" people's houses. You're an interior designer.'

She nodded.

'Why didn't you say?' he added.

Good question. Esme couldn't remember the answer.

'You seemed to be enjoying jumping to other conclusions,' she declared at length.

He looked askance at her but didn't argue. Instead he began to leaf through her portfolio of sketches. 'How long have you been doing this?'

'Design work—about three years,' she replied. 'This particular commission—a few weeks. Although it seems a lot longer.'

'Problems?' he enquired.

She shrugged. What did he care? She gathered up her work, slipping it back in its case, and, with a vague wave of the hand, invited him to sit down.

He took the sofa, shrugging off his jacket to drape it across the back.

Esme sat on an easy chair, carefully arranging the folds of her robe, before pouring the tea.

'I was wondering,' he continued when she'd handed him a cup, 'if you've time to do some work for me...on the design front, I mean.'

The latter was added in case Esme imagined he was touting for a cleaner.

She still didn't know what to say. 'I—I... At Highfield?' Stupid question! Where else?

He nodded. 'The builders are still renovating the framework of the house, but it'll eventually need to be furnished and decorated from top to bottom.'

'But why me?' she asked.

'Why not you?' he countered. 'You know Highfield and I suspect you're more likely to do something sympathetic to the style and age of the house.'

Esme was tempted. A project like Highfield was a designer's dream. But, realistically, could she manage it?

'I've only ever worked on a single-room basis,' she admitted. 'You might be better off with a bigger firm.'

'I've had a couple in already.' He grimaced. 'Country home meets New York loft.'

'Minimalist?' The style was currently flavour of the month.

'Bare is the word I'd use,' he responded, 'although, to be fair, I gave them pretty minimal instruction. I assumed they'd do something in keeping with the period of the house.'

She shook her head. 'You have to state some preferences or most designers will treat your house as a work of art rather than a place to live.'

'Well,' he responded, 'I don't like anything too flowery, I don't like pastels, I don't like light-coloured wood or pine or reproduction furniture. Is that sufficient brief?'

'It's a start,' Esme agreed, although it was a more negative than positive indication of his taste.

'So when could you?'

'What?'

'Start.'

Was this why he was here? No, he had only just discovered that she did interior design. It had to be a spur-of-the-moment request.

It would have been easy to accept it on the same basis but she couldn't ignore the drawbacks. For her to work for him would require trust on both sides and that was certainly absent.

'I couldn't,' she replied at length. 'I haven't the time or the manpower.'

'Or the inclination?' he added astutely.

Esme declined to answer, saying instead, 'You wanted to discuss the tenancy?'

His lips quirked but he let her change the subject. 'I understand you're concerned about the security of your tenure.'

An understatement. Her eyes went to his face, trying to read the unreadable.

'So what's this—pay-off time?' she asked, referring back to an earlier conversation.

Jack frowned briefly, then remembered. 'Would that be your preference—a financial settlement?'

Esme, who'd been joking, stared at him in surprise. Would he really do that? Give her money to leave? It seemed so.

She didn't hide her disdain. 'I don't want money from you. If I decide to move, it'll be because I want to.'

'Perhaps you'd better tell Harry that, then,' he countered, an edge to his voice now.

She bristled at his use of her son's name. 'What do you mean?'

He slipped a hand inside the suit jacket he was wearing. 'Here.'

He extended a folded piece of paper. She took it with reluctance.

It was a moment before she fathomed it was a printout of an e-mail. She read it quickly, then more slowly, with a growing sense of disbelief.

'You've been communicating with my son?' She didn't have to feign outrage.

'No, he's been communicating with me,' he qualified. 'I merely acknowledged receipt.'

'But how?' How could Harry have sent this—an appeal for Jack Doyle not to throw them out of the cottage?

'By using considerable initiative, I'd say,' the man relayed. 'It seems he talked to Jones, the builder, who referred him to Rebecca—the wife of my partner; you might remember meeting her—who, with a little persuasion, gave him my e-mail address...I assume he has access to a computer.'

'He has one in his bedroom,' she confirmed.

'With a modem?' he enquired, and, at her uncertain look, added, 'Is it connected up to the internet?'

She nodded. 'He uses it for homework, sometimes, but the company who installed it told me they'd put a block on it so he couldn't go into chat rooms or receive any inappropriate material.'

Esme fell silent, wondering why she was justifying herself to him. It wasn't as if he were any better a parent. He wasn't one full stop.

'It wouldn't stop him *sending* e-mails,' he explained, 'and I suspect Harry is smart enough to get round any blocking procedures if he chose... Still, no harm's been done this time.'

If that was meant to mollify Esme, it missed its mark by a mile. No harm? An as-good-as-begging letter to their landlord. And what about *his* response?

'What did you tell him?' she demanded next.

'I can't remember exactly,' he replied, 'but you'll probably find it still on his hard drive, if you care to *vet* it.'

Esme might have leapt up and done just that if she'd known how, but computers were largely foreign territory to her. Not that she was about to admit it.

'The basic gist,' he continued at her silence, 'was not to worry, your tenancy was assured and I'd clear things up when I returned.'

'How magnanimous of you!' Now Harry would think that any future move was down to her.

The sarcasm drew a quizzical look from Jack, before he worked things out for himself. 'I get it. You wanted to leave and I was a convenient excuse. And if the boy thinks I'm a wicked landlord, who cares?'

He obviously did and Esme had the grace to blush. She couldn't make any denial—so she didn't.

'Have you found somewhere else?'

'Not yet.'

'But you're looking?'

Esme studied her hands as she nodded.

'Why exactly?' he asked, then answered for himself, 'This thing between you and me?'

His bluntness had her head jerking upwards. Mistake. Grey eyes met and locked on hers.

She wanted to say, *Thing?* as if she hadn't the first clue what he meant. She would have if she'd felt she could be convincing. But the *thing* had stirred into life the moment she'd seen him again and, under his steady gaze, was now bashing away at its cage door.

'Everything isn't about you, Jack Doyle,' she retaliated instead. 'I've been buried away here for the best part of eight years and it's time I moved on.'

She was conscious of speaking in clichés but managed to make it sound heartfelt.

'I can't argue with that,' he countered, 'but are you sure a flat above a Chinese takeaway in Southbury is the way to go?'

She cursed Harry. Was nothing sacred?

'It's what I can afford,' she justified before glancing back down at the e-mail in her hand. 'How did you know about that, anyway? It isn't on here.'

He hesitated before admitting, 'Harry was on-line when I e-mailed him last night.'

So they'd had a nice little chat, Esme concluded, taking a dimmer and dimmer view of the wonders of modern technology.

'I'm sorry if you don't approve, but—'

'What's not to approve?' she cut across him. 'Other than the fact my son spends his evenings revealing our personal lives to a virtual stranger.'

'Come on, Esme, I'm no stranger,' Jack cajoled, 'and the boy was acting in what he saw as your interests. You can't blame him for that.'

He clearly imagined she was going to punish Harry in some way. Perhaps she would—or pull the plug on his computer for a while, at least. But whatever she did was none of Jack Doyle's business.

She told him as much, saying, 'I'll deal with Harry how I see fit,' before rising from her seat.

He was quick, following suit so he effectively blocked her way to the door. 'Look, I didn't come here to get the boy into trouble. He's a great kid. A credit to you. I know it can't be easy, raising the boy on your own.'

Esme didn't hear the compliment, just what she considered his patronising tone. Her resentment spilled over. 'As if you care.'

She cringed at her own words. They could have come from a five-year-old. Perhaps that was why he showed forbearance.

'Actually, I do care.' He gazed down at her, willing her to look up at him, before he said, 'Why else do you think I'm here? I want to help you.'

His concern sounded genuine but Esme saw something quite different in his eyes. Did he really take her for a fool? 'You want to sleep with me, you mean.'

Jack contemplated denial, then he remembered how she'd been in his head all the time he'd been away. Maybe it was good that they didn't play games.

'That as well,' he agreed at length, 'but it isn't a prerequisite. I'll help you, regardless.'

Esme remained sceptical. 'So I tell you now that I'm never going to bed with you and ask for, let's say, some money as deposit on a decent flat, you're going to give it to me?'

It was a rhetorical question, not intended seriously at all.

Esme was aghast when he barely hesitated before reaching for his jacket from the back of the sofa and going into the inside pocket for his wallet.

'How much?' he said simply.

'I don't want your money!' she threw back. 'That was a "what if." God, you must think I'm desperate.'

'I think you're broke,' he corrected.

'Well, I'm not!' she refuted. 'And even if I was, you couldn't buy me.'

From the darkening of his expression, she'd finally managed to hit a nerve.

'That wasn't my intention. And from memory,' he responded coldly, 'I don't need to buy you.'

Esme's face flamed even as she hissed back, 'You bastard!'

'Probably,' he agreed.

'I was sixteen and I was drunk—' she was tired of his holding the past over her '—and I wouldn't consider yourself irresistible because of it.'

'And last month, last week—' he caught her arm when she made to walk past him '—were you drunk then? You certainly aren't sixteen any more.'

Esme didn't waste energy trying to twist free but she went on the offensive, all the same. 'No, you're right. I'm a twenty-six-year-old single mother who hasn't slept with a man in years and, as such, *is* probably on the desperate side. Not much of a challenge, that, is it?'

She meant to annoy, ridicule, send him in retreat, but he suddenly looked pleased with himself.

'Interesting,' he remarked. 'So what are you and Charles waiting for? The wedding night?'

Esme was stopped in her tracks. She'd forgotten she'd mentioned Charles to him.

'Would that be so awful? Charles is a gentleman.'

He said nothing, but made a sound of disgust that couldn't possibly be ignored.

'Not that I'd expect *you* to appreciate such a quality,' she added meaningfully.

'You're right, I don't.' He dragged her round to face him. 'I'm just the cook son's, remember? Not some bloody sexless, upper-class twit... But, yes, it would be awful, married to someone who can actually *wait* to make love to you, doesn't long to take you to bed, hear you cry out as he—'

'Stop it!' Too much truth for Esme to bear. 'Why are you doing this?'

'You know why.' He tried to gather her closer but she warded him off, placing a hand against the wall of his chest.

Beneath it, she felt the beating of his heart, wild as hers. 'You need me to tell you?'

A threat, softly spoken.

She shook her head. No more words.

They would only compound the way he made her feel, his eyes burning into hers, slowly destroying her will.

So why keep looking at him? Why let him grasp her hands and lead her back towards the fire? Stay still as a statue while he framed her face in his hands to place a first tender kiss on her cheek?

She had shut her eyes by then so he no longer had the power to make her do things, yet it was she who raised her head and, like a starving soul, sought his mouth.

He fed her hunger with his cool breath and his bruising lips and the warm thrust of his tongue, but she wanted more. They fell on the sofa together, and, from there, rolled onto the hearth rug to lie by the dying fire. She needed his hands, caressing, touching, pushing inside silk and cotton to her breasts, fondling till they were heavy and full. No protest made when he untied the belt, spreading the robe, the night-gown beneath. She reached for him, too, carelessly ripping buttons off his shirt, palms gliding through rough male hair already slick with sweat.

She lay for him as he moved his head downwards, lips to the base of her throat, the hollows of her shoulder, the rise of her breasts, inexorably downwards until finally they opened on the hard nipple thrust eagerly into his mouth.

She needed this. Needed it like food or water. Wanted it more.

Greedy as he. One breast, then the other. Aching for it. Tongue, gently nuzzling, now teeth, teasing and biting, drawing whimpers from her breathless throat.

A question asked. Head shaken. No, no protection.

Never mind. This time for her. Lie back, darling.

Not really understanding. Mouth back on a nipple. Hand on her belly. Sliding over the curve. Seeking, pushing. Suddenly inside her thighs. Making her flinch. Soothing.

Stroking. Parting those other lips. Long fingers, in and out, strong and rhythmic, until she was panting hard.

Stopping then. Breast abandoned. His head moving downwards. Her hips gently raised. A mouth placed where his fingers had been, a tongue lapping, serving her so unfamiliarly she cried out. Then shuddering, coming, in a gush of warm, wet pleasure.

Left drained and satisfied but shaking as he wrapped her back in the soft folds of the robe. Unable to look at him. Shamed by her very surrender.

'OK?' A curiously tender kiss was placed on her temple.

She nodded but kept her eyes tight shut in case he saw too much. No man had ever brought her to fulfilment that way. It was almost as if she'd lost her innocence again.

'Next time—' he pushed a strand of hair from her face '—I'll come prepared.'

Finally she opened her eyes.

He gazed at her possessively, not hiding what was in his thoughts.

She half wished he would do it now. Take her and be done with it. She knew she owed him.

She could have left it, picked a better time, but Esme felt compelled to be honest. She sat up, clutching her robe to her, as she finally responded, 'I'm sorry but there won't be a next time.'

'What?' Clearly stunned, he sat up, too, and caught her arm, forcing her round. 'What are you saying?'

'I don't want you coming round again.' She couldn't stand it—a relationship dominated by sex from which he could walk away whenever he pleased.

'But—' his eyes raked her face and saw she was serious '—what was all that about?'

She read it as a kind of accusation, perhaps one she deserved. She'd let him make love to her without giving much in return and now here she was, finishing it.

'You want to do it properly.' She spoke her earlier thoughts aloud. 'I won't stop you, but that's it.'

She couldn't have him coming and going as he pleased. She knew she wouldn't cope with it.

'*You won't stop me?*' he echoed her choice of words. 'Is that intended as a turn-on or a turn-off?'

'I…no…I—I just m-meant…' She stammered at the sudden fury in his face.

'Forget it!' He pushed her away from him. 'I know what you meant. A favour for a favour. Well, no, thanks.'

He was on his feet, shoving his unbuttoned shirt into his trousers and grabbing for his jacket before she had the chance to say anything in reply.

She had what she wanted. He was heading for the door. So why did she follow?

She caught him up in the hall and grabbed at his sleeve before he could leave. 'You don't understand.'

'Don't I?' he growled back. 'Well, why don't you come and explain it to me some time? Maybe when you're feeling a little frustrated and in need of some male company. Who knows? If I'm desperate enough, I may just oblige.'

'It wasn't like that!' Esme protested, between tears and temper.

'Wasn't it?' His eyes blazed with contempt.

He had never looked at Esme like that before. It tore holes in her heart even as she threw back, 'You were the one who came to me.'

'More fool me, then,' he growled and, roughly setting her aside, dragged open the door.

He left it wide as he strode off into the darkness.

Esme slammed it shut, a final gesture of defiance, before she collapsed into a crying, pathetic heap.

What had she done?

CHAPTER SIX

WHAT had she done?

She woke the next day asking herself the same question, and unfortunately remembered the answer all too well as she drifted through to the living room. The fire was dead, just ash in the grate—much as she felt inside. Passion burned out, leaving only waste behind.

Or more accurately shame. That she could be so weak. How could she ever face Jack Doyle again?

She seriously contemplated running: abandoning her belongings and just driving away.

To where? That was the problem. Her mother's. God, no. But who else would take her in?

She thought of Charles, and rejected him in almost the same instant, just as the telephone rang.

She stared at it hard for a moment, as if she could guess the identity of the ringer, then told herself to stop being silly. Whoever it was, it wouldn't be Jack Doyle. He had made it quite clear that she'd have to come running to him.

She picked it up and murmured a tentative, 'Yes?'

'Esme?' a male voice enquired.

'Yes. Hi, Charles,' she said with some relief.

'I know you're busy at the moment—' he repeated the last excuse she'd used on him '—but I wondered if you were free tonight. We could go out for a meal.'

Esme heard the diffident note in his voice. She had to do something. It wasn't fair to keep him dangling.

'Why don't you come here, Charles? I'll make us something.' She felt a let-down might be easier over dinner at home.

'I...well...' Charles was clearly surprised. 'Are you sure? I don't want to put you to any trouble.'

'No trouble,' Esme assured him but she was already re-

gretting the impulse. Had that been a note of hope in
Charles's voice? 'Say, eight o'clock. Phone me from the car
and I'll come down and open the gates. They're on a remote-
control system now.'

'Ah, the new broom,' Charles joked. 'So, what's he like?'

'I don't really know,' lied Esme. 'Listen, I'm going to have
to go. I'll see you tonight.'

'All right,' he signed off. 'Looking forward to it.'

Esme replaced the receiver and pulled a face. There was
no mistaking the warmth in Charles's goodbye. He had no
idea why she'd asked him here.

Not that she had to worry about his behaviour. She would
let him down gently and he would accept it. No caveman
tactics from him. He really was the perfect gentleman.

So why couldn't she want him?

Esme suspected the answer lay in some defect in her own
nature. Still, she was fighting it, and at least she was now
mature enough not to go dressing up her feelings.

She blushed for her sixteen-year-old self. How guileless
that girl had been. Adoring Jack Doyle as if he were God's
gift.

True, he had been good-looking. *Still was,* an insidious
voice chimed in. And, yes, he had been kind, noticing her
artistic talents and insisting she was smart despite her erratic
spelling and even greater difficulties with maths.

But then, hadn't her father paid him to tutor her during
several school holidays? Hadn't praising her been just part
of the deal?

Well, she was older and wiser now and she didn't remember him saying anything particularly kind last night. Maybe
about Harry, but that had been more in the nature of an *isn't
he a great kid despite being brought up by a single mother*
type remark.

And hadn't she lived down to his expectations? She
cringed when she thought of it. More than ten years passed
and she was still letting him mess her about. At least there
would be no long-term consequences this time.

Which led her on to thinking of Harry and how she was

going to tackle the subject of e-mailing virtual strangers. He'd been trying to help and she didn't want to make a huge issue of it, but he had to realise: they were moving from the cottage, regardless.

She'd prepared a speech for when she picked him up later from his friend Adam's house, but he was so buoyant she was reluctant to destroy his good mood. It seemed Adam's dad had taken them out to something called Laser Quest which was terribly cool. Esme listened patiently to a blow-by-blow account, before offering to take him back there some time.

Harry pulled a slight face. 'It's kind of boys' stuff, Mum.'

He didn't mean to be hurtful, and normally Esme would have laughed off such a sexist comment, but today it made her feel inadequate. Try as she might, she was never going to make up for one lack in Harry's life—a father.

Which brought her back to Jack. Not that she was about to go in for any true confessions. OK, so Harry had liked Jack enough to e-mail him a begging letter, and Jack had responded in a friendly manner. But that was a far cry from Jack welcoming a son he'd never asked for and Harry deserved better than a reluctant father.

'Um…what did you do last night, Mum?' Harry went on to ask.

For a moment Esme thought he was making up for his dismissive remark and answered vaguely, 'Oh, you know. A bit of work. Watched some TV.'

'Oh.' Harry sounded disappointed.

She added, 'Tonight, though, Charles is coming round. I'm cooking him a meal.'

'Right.' Harry was clearly underwhelmed. 'I don't have to be there, do I?'

'No.' Esme was relieved he'd counted himself out, but still added, 'I thought you liked Charles.'

'He's OK,' Harry agreed flatly, 'but he does ask stupid questions.'

'Like what?' Esme hadn't noticed.

'Like, ''How are you doing at school?'' And, ''Do you

play rugby?'' And even, ''What do you want for Christmas?''' Harry relayed, 'when it's only Easter.'

Esme might have laughed in sympathy if she hadn't felt guilty about her own treatment of Charles. 'He's just trying to make conversation.'

'Boring,' Harry dismissed, to Esme's further annoyance.

'Maybe he should e-mail you instead,' she threw back. 'You seem to prefer that. Quite a little chatterbox on the computer, I've heard.'

It sounded like what it was, an accusation. She wished it unsaid almost instantly. So much for her resolution to tackle the matter calmly.

She half hoped that Harry wouldn't pick up on the implication but she'd forgotten how quick he was.

A brief silence followed before he said, 'Jack came to see you.'

Esme considered feigning ignorance. Now hardly felt the right time to talk about this. But it was an opening.

'If you mean Mr Doyle,' she confirmed, 'Then, yes, he came last night.'

Harry sneaked a glance at her face, noted the tightness around her mouth. 'You're mad, aren't you?'

Completely crazy, yes, when she considered her encounter with Jack, but that wasn't what Harry meant.

'No, not really,' she replied heavily, then went on to contradict it by saying, 'Ignoring the fact that we agreed you would *never* use your computer to communicate with total strangers—'

'He isn't!'

'Don't interrupt,' she rebuked. 'He is virtually.'

'But he used to live in our cottage,' Harry reasoned. 'You knew him when you were little.'

'That is not the point I'm making.' Esme grew more exasperated. 'If I'd wanted you to go begging I'd have sent you in person, shoeless and cap in hand. But I don't, so I'd appreciate it if you didn't talk to him again.'

A longer silence followed. It was Esme's turn to glance in Harry's direction. She thought she'd really upset him with her snappy tone. But, no, she knew that expression: stubborn resistance.

'On the computer,' he asked, 'or at all?'

When had he become so pedantic? Or was she only just noticing the trait? She knew its origin, having had a recent update of the adult version.

The words 'at all' were on her lips but she didn't say them. She couldn't. The day would come when talking to his father—so far a nebulous character—might be of primary importance to him. Would he remember then how she had forbidden it? Would he even forgive her for keeping the truth from him?

She sloughed away from the subject now. 'It hardly matters. We'll be moving on soon,' she said with quiet authority.

She tensed for further argument. None came.

Instead Harry muttered, *'He said,'* and this time the disappointed anger wasn't directed at her.

She had a choice: the truth or the easy way out? She picked the latter, and, in the silence that developed, tried to justify it. What did it matter if Harry thought the man had let him down? She was the one who had to live with him, the one who had to bring him up. Jack Doyle should have never made promises he couldn't keep.

'Here.' She tried to hand Harry the remote control as they approached the gates.

It was still a novelty, pressing the button to make the gates open. Or it had been.

He refused with a brusque, 'No, thanks.'

She kept any irritation to herself and operated the remote. It took several clicks before anything happened and she scowled at the little gadget.

When they finally reached the cottage and went inside Harry would have immediately disappeared upstairs if she hadn't stopped him.

'Look, Harry—' she silently cursed her excess of conscience '—you should know. It has nothing to do with Jack Doyle. He'd let us stay if we wanted to.'

'But,' Harry struggled to work out what was going on, 'if that's the case, why…?'

'I realise it's hard for you to understand,' she sighed in reply, 'but I feel it's time for both of us to move on. It's not good for either of us, on our own here, just you and me, so isol—'

'I want to go to my room,' he interrupted, for once sounding younger than his years.

Esme was a little shocked at his rudeness, but she saw behind it to how upset he was. She put out a hand, meaning to give him a cuddle, but he brushed her off, making for the stairs to take them two at a time.

She could have followed but what to say? She had changed her mind? She hadn't. It would all work out for the best? A platitude. She believed it, though.

She let well alone until later that afternoon, when she brought him up tea of sandwiches, milk and apple.

He was on his computer. No surprise there. Was this enough to eat? Yes, thank you. Did he want to talk? If she wanted to. How did he feel? Fine.

Esme managed not to lose her temper. After all, he was being polite enough, just monosyllabic. She decided to concentrate her energies on preparing the meal for Charles.

She made less effort on her appearance, changing from jeans and sweatshirt to simple trousers and a polo neck.

Charles phoned from the gates and she went down, once again taking several clicks on the device to open them.

She waved Charles through and, after more frantic clicking, managed to shut the gates. Why couldn't Doyle have just let the old ones alone?

She climbed into the car with Charles and wasn't quick enough to avoid the kiss he placed on her mouth. Pleasant enough, but it left her determined. Tonight was the night. She had to finish things.

It was hard, especially when Charles said and did nothing to suggest that he now wanted a relationship beyond friendship until they reached coffee and liqueurs and he suddenly slid an arm across the back of the sofa.

'Cream!' she exclaimed, grabbing the flimsiest of excuses to escape.

She disappeared to the kitchen and counted out ten seconds before returning empty-handed. 'Sorry, all out of it!'

'Don't worry,' a bemused Charles assured her, 'I don't actually take cream.'

'Don't you?' Esme managed to make this sound like a newly discovered fact. 'It just shows, doesn't it—we don't really know that much about each other?'

A start! she applauded herself while making sure to sit back down on the single armchair.

'We know the important things.' Charles smiled back. 'I mean we come from similar backgrounds, like the same things...opera, the ballet, the hunt.'

Esme's heart sank. That sounded like the beginning of a speech, one he'd rehearsed a few times.

'Not totally, no.' She decided dissension was called for, 'I've never really liked hunting. It's always struck me as a little barbaric, horses and hounds chasing one poor fox.'

Now surely that was sacrilege to an ardent countryman like Charles?

'Yes, well—' he smiled indulgently '—that's a matter of opinion, although any farmer will tell you what a pest the foxes are... Still, I admire your stance.'

Esme sighed inwardly. She didn't want him admiring her stance. She wanted him to open his eyes and see how vastly unsuited they were.

'Anyway, I meant horsemanship generally,' he continued in his dogged way. 'You were such a brilliant jumper, I remember. You really should take it up again. You could use one of my horses.'

'Thanks, but I'm usually too busy.' Esme smiled to soften her refusal. 'With work and everything.'

'At the moment, yes,' he conceded, 'but if your life were different... Which is really what I'm trying to say. I'd like to make it so. In fact, I came here hoping we might discuss the future—'

'Charles—' Esme had a premonition of what he was about

to say and intended to stop him at all costs '—it's very nice of you, but I've already made some plans. I want to grow the business and move—probably to London in the longer term. That's where the work is.'

'I...oh...right.' This information threw Charles completely. 'I didn't realise you were so serious about this decorating lark.'

Esme could have said it was design, not decorating, and work, not a lark, but it wasn't Charles's fault that he was stuck in a time warp where girls only worked as a hobby before marriage.

'Totally serious,' Esme stressed, 'which is why I wanted to talk to you tonight. You've been great, taking me out and about and treating me, but you deserve better. Someone more focused on you... And, between my career commitments and Harry, that's never going to be me,' she finished gently as his face finally reflected disappointed resignation.

'No,' he agreed at length, 'I see that now and I appreciate your honesty.'

Esme yearned to reply, *Don't be nice. Get mad for once. Stand up for yourself. Tell me I'm a bitch.*

But it would be perverse when she'd just negotiated a minefield to gain this quiet acceptance rather than a slanging match.

She settled for a prosaic, 'Want some more coffee?'

A cue, and Charles for once took it, looking at his watch to exclaim, 'Is that the time? No, I'm afraid I'll have to go. Cricket match tomorrow.'

'Right.' She rose and he followed. 'I'll get a jacket and take you down to the gates.'

They busied themselves with finding car keys and an umbrella, because the hot summer's day had given way to another storm, and took refuge in typically English conversation about weather till they reached the gates and discovered they wouldn't open at all.

'It's either your device or the gates.' Charles stated the obvious. 'We'll have to call the main house. I think there's an intercom by the side of that pillar.'

He was out of the car before Esme could stop him. Maybe it was better, she decided, letting Charles do the talking.

Or maybe not, as Charles returned to declare, 'Odd chap. I told him who I was but he insists on verification from you.'

Esme sighed loudly. 'OK, I'll deal with it.'

Forgetting the umbrella, she braved the storm and impatiently buzzed the intercom button.

'Yes?' a disembodied voice enquired.

'It's me.'

'You?'

'*Esme.*'

'Yes?'

Esme gritted her teeth. 'My clicky thingummy seems to be on the blink.'

'Clicky thingummy?' he repeated in dry, mocking tones. 'And that would be the technical term for what, precisely?'

'My—' what was the word again? '—remote. It's ceased functioning,' she added for good measure.

'Have you dropped it at all?' he asked next.

'No. Why, would that help it work again?'

'Is that a joke?'

More in the nature of sarcasm at his suggestion *she* must have done something wrong. Perhaps unwise in the circumstances.

'Well, this isn't,' she retorted crossly. 'It's raining and I'm getting wet, so if you could just come down here and do something. Charles would like to go home.'

'On his own?' Unbelievable.

'Is that any of your business?' she seethed.

'Is last night any business of his?' he countered.

Was that a threat? To tell Charles what had happened between them?

It scarcely mattered now her relationship with Charles had ended, but she didn't want Charles hurt, thinking he was being dumped for someone else.

'I forgot—he's the jealous type,' Jack resumed. 'Well, don't worry, it'll be our little secret.'

He was mocking her and, realising it, Esme muttered a

careless, 'Oh, go to hell!' before she noticed the gates were finally opening.

She half expected them to shut again. When they didn't, she hurried back to the car. She didn't climb in but went to the driver's side.

Charles, having already wound his window down, looked at her with concern. 'You're soaked.'

'I'll be fine.' She took the umbrella he handed her and unfurled it.

'He seems an awkward devil,' Charles added. 'Is that why you're moving?'

'One of the reasons.' She glanced towards the gates. 'You'd better not hang around. He might shut them again.'

Charles nodded before saying, 'Well, look after yourself, Esme.'

'You, too.' She leaned inside the car and kissed him briefly on the cheek. 'Thanks for everything.'

It was goodbye. They both knew that. Esme didn't prolong it as she backed away from the car.

She waited until he'd swept through the gates before buzzing once more on the intercom.

'You can close them again,' she informed Jack coldly.

'Has he gone?' was his curt response.

'Yes.'

'Good.'

Good? What was that—approval?

Esme scowled as she walked away and the gates closed behind her. She wondered if she was going to have to go through the Spanish Inquisition every time she wanted to leave Highfield.

She shook her head. He surely wouldn't want the hassle, either.

Back at the cottage, she changed into her night clothes, towel-dried her hair, then went to wash the dinner dishes, cursing Jack Doyle and his useless security gates.

Still, she'd done what she'd set out to do—disentangled herself from Charles without too much upset. She might have felt guilty: she was almost sure Charles had been leading up to a proposal. But surely the ease with which he had been diverted said it all? Had he truly wanted her, would he have given up at the first hurdle?

Her mind wandered involuntarily to Jack Doyle. She couldn't imagine him meekly accepting a turn-down if he wanted something or someone. Even with Arabella he hadn't given up because of the terrible things their mother had said, but rather the realisation that she was just a mouthpiece: that it was Arabella who hadn't considered him good enough for her. And he hadn't reacted with disappointment but fury. She knew that well enough because she'd received the backlash, albeit turned into a different kind of passion.

That she'd asked for it did not make it feel any better. She'd allowed herself to play second best to Arabella, perpetuating the whole pattern of their childhood.

Well, that was then and this was now. She was out of her sister's shadow, had been for years. On the rare occasions she met up with her she could make meaningless small talk without feeling anything worse than boredom and certainly never envy, recognising her own life as happier, more meaningful.

Yet she was still regressing, devaluing all her efforts to leave the old Esme behind.

OK, she wasn't falling over Jack Doyle like an over-eager puppy. Or hanging on to his words of wisdom any more. Or mooning around, wondering if he'd ever notice her. She'd opened her eyes and seen him for what he was—a clever, arrogant, good-looking bastard. Yet she'd succumbed.

Why? was the question. She forced herself to think back to last night. He'd come to talk about the tenancy and Harry's e-mails, ostensibly to offer his help. She'd thrown it back in his face, suggesting he was trying to buy her. He'd pointed out he'd never had to do that, alluding to their encounter in the barn, and things had degenerated from there.

She should have shown him the door. Why hadn't she? She'd tried to retaliate and somehow they'd ended up talking about sex. She remembered being both repelled and fascinated, like watching a blue movie. Then suddenly she'd been starring in her very own one, only she was honest enough to admit there had been nothing phony about her moans and groans and the climax he'd given her.

Esme felt herself trembling, and quickly shut off the projector in her head. She had her answer. It was need. Quite simple, if rather shameful. She had needed sex. After three years' celibacy and emotional detachment, her body had betrayed her.

That it had been with Jack Doyle didn't hold any great, mystical significance. He had been there. That was all. He had been there and suddenly familiar, as if it was meant to be, and he was good at it, very good, and she'd weakened. End of story.

She just had to face up to it. She wasn't as self-contained as she'd imagined. She was like many single mothers, putting children and work first, learning to live with loneliness, emotions firmly on hold, until some man came along—often wrong but timing right—to breach their defences.

She told herself it wouldn't happen again but that errant voice inside her just laughed back, *Who are you kidding?*

She would have argued with it but it sounded so certain. And, anyway, it was late and she was tired.

She trudged upstairs, checked on Harry, fast asleep, then trudged back down to her room off the hall and fell into bed to toss and turn until exhaustion won out.

The storm died out by early morning. She slept through her alarm clock ringing and the sun filtering through half-drawn curtains, only to be aroused by knocking on the cottage door.

It took her a moment to gain full consciousness, glance at the time—ten o'clock—then scramble for clothes.

Already too late as she heard the bolt being shot and the sound of voices in conversation. Impossible not to hear, with her room just off the hall.

She'd pulled on a sweatshirt and was dragging up her jeans when Harry said, 'Maybe you could persuade her.'

'I don't think so somehow,' Jack replied. 'Anyway, she may be right. It is very isolated here.'

'Better than town,' was Harry's opinion. 'If I go there, I'll never get away from them.'

Esme stopped in her tracks. Was Harry that miserable at school?

'Them?' Jack asked the question on her lips.

'Kids at school.'

'Bullies?'

No answer came but Esme guessed Harry was either nodding or shaking his head.

Nodding, it seemed, as Jack resumed, 'Yeah, that stuff happens if you're different.'

'Did it happen to you?' Harry wondered aloud.

'Off and on,' Jack confirmed.

'What did you do?' asked Harry.

'Well, I'd like to give you some magic solution,' Jack responded in his slightly Americanised drawl, 'but I'm afraid there isn't one. You could tell your teacher.'

'Done that.'

'Not very effective?'

'She says I should try to fit in and make friends with them.'

'Great,' the man applauded sarcastically. 'Is that before or after they beat you up?

Harry laughed, as intended, before volunteering, 'During, maybe.'

'Have you told your mother?' Jack suggested next.

'She knows they call me names and stuff,' Harry confided, 'but if I tell her how serious it is she'll just go up to the school and make a fuss and then I'll be in even more trouble.'

'I can see your point,' Jack agreed, 'but they're not going to stop until someone stops them. You should speak to your mother... Where is she, by the way?'

'In bed.' Harry betrayed her without thought. 'I'll get her.'

He knocked on Esme's door and she called out, 'Be out in a moment,' as she pulled a brush through her hair and finally made her entrance into the hall.

'Go help yourself to breakfast,' she directed at Harry, 'while I speak to Mr Doyle.'

When Harry had departed, she turned to the man on the

doorstep. He was dressed in white T-shirt and black jeans, freshly shaven and coolly handsome. Esme felt at an immediate disadvantage and wished she hadn't just grabbed the first clothes to hand, her scruffiest jeans and a grubby old sweatshirt.

'Yes?' She dispensed with niceties.

'I've brought a replacement remote.' He handed over the new device. 'That's the only spare, so if I could have the faulty device?'

'Of course.' She opened a drawer in the hall cabinet where she'd put it for safe-keeping.

'Thanks.' He nodded as if about to depart, then thought better of it. 'Look, I was just talking to Harry...'

'I know—I heard.'

'Right.'

'I'll deal with it,' she stated abruptly.

He continued to stand there. She stared back at him, daring him to dispense unwelcome advice.

But either he had the sense not to or he didn't care, because he suddenly switched subjects on her. 'About last night, I was being difficult. I admit it. I suspect I took exception to your friend's tone.'

Esme's brows drew together. Charles only had one tone.

'Which was?' she demanded curtly. 'I've never known Charles to be anything less than polite.'

'Maybe it was that then.' He made a face. 'Upper-class English superciliousness, scrupulously polite with just a hint of condescension.'

'Whereas your tone is what?' Esme couldn't resist retorting. 'Working-class-boy-done-good with just a hint of chip-on-shoulder.'

He laughed. He actually laughed. Didn't he know when someone was insulting him?

'And you?' He held his head at an angle. 'Let's see... English lady, seemingly so remote and untouchable, but underneath—'

'Was there anything else you wanted?' she interrupted, somewhat unwisely.

It gave him the chance to murmur, 'I think we both know I want something else but it'll have to keep for now. I'm leaving for Tokyo in the morning. Any more trouble with the gates and you should speak to Colin Jones, the builder. He'll be working on the house.'

She listened to this information with a mixture of feelings. She should feel relief and she did. But there was also a sense that he was abandoning her once more. Definitely odd.

'Your rent?' Esme reminded them both of their current relationship. 'I can give you a cheque.'

'No rush,' he replied. 'I'll be back in a few days.'

'If that suits.' She wasn't going to argue.

He inclined his head. 'Say goodbye to Harry for me.'

'OK.'

'Tell him…'

'What?'

She frowned, unsure if she wanted any dialogue between the two.

He shrugged before suggesting, 'Tell him it gets better.'

'Right.' She wondered if he was speaking from experience.

'See you, then.' Already walking away, he raised his hand in a farewell salute.

Esme had no need to echo, 'See you,' but she did, which was probably why he turned briefly and slanted her a smile.

No. More of a grin. Did he imagine he was wearing her down?

Well, he wasn't, and to prove it she awarded him a positive scowl.

It didn't seem to bother him as he went up the path, hands in pockets, whistling.

She closed the door with a slight bang and passed through the living room to the kitchen beyond.

'Has he gone?' Harry looked up from his breakfast.

'Mr Doyle? Yes.'

'You could have invited him in.'

Esme raised a brow—this, from the most antisocial boy in the world.

'He was in a hurry,' she lied. 'He's off to Tokyo.'

'Cool,' Harry approved, Japan being the Mecca of all things high-tec. 'Did he say when he's coming back?'

'No.' Esme lied again, but for some reason felt compelled to admit, 'He wanted me to tell you goodbye and that "it gets better"…if you know what he means.'

'Life, I suppose,' concluded Harry, quite the little philosopher. 'He was bullied at school. Jack…Mr Doyle, I mean. He understands.'

And she didn't? Esme bit back the retort. This wasn't about the war between Jack and her.

'I heard you talking,' Esme admitted. 'How bad is it really?'

Harry pulled a face. 'When they call me posh geek and boff and stuff like that I try to ignore them, like you said, but that only seems to make them madder.'

'Are they hitting you?'

'Sometimes. Kicking, mostly. Or body-punching in the dinner line when the supervisors are looking away.'

'Oh, Harry, we have to tell someone!' Esme had had no idea things had deteriorated to this point.

'I've tried—' Harry's face suffused with temper, not against her but the injustice of the world '—but the moment I put my hand up they either thump me in the back or they put their hands up, too, and shout out that *I've* kicked *them* and then *I* get into trouble.'

Oh, God. What to do? Esme's first inclination was to take Harry out of the school forthwith, but where did he go then? And what guarantee was there that it wouldn't happen again?

'I'll have to go in and speak to your teacher, darling.' Esme caught the look of consternation on his face. 'I know you don't want me to, but what else can we do?'

Harry shook his head adamantly before quoting, 'Jack says it'll get better.'

'Not the bullying, he didn't.' Esme was sure of that. 'What he actually said was, they're not going to stop until someone stops them. And it's been going on a while, hasn't it?'

Harry didn't deny it, but implored instead, 'Please, Mum,

don't go in. It'll be the holidays in a few weeks and most of the bullies will leave for high school.'

Esme found herself wavering. He clearly hated the idea of her fighting his battles for him.

'Please, Mum.' Solemn grey eyes held hers in entreaty.

How familiar were those eyes now! All those years denying someone else had helped make this child and here she was, confronted with the truth of it.

'OK, but—' she began to lay down conditions.

Harry, however, drowned her out with a heartfelt, 'Thanks, Mum, you're the best,' and gave her one of his hard hugs.

She returned the hug but her unease remained, a premonition of events to come.

CHAPTER SEVEN

THE week passed uneventfully. Harry claimed the bullies had lost interest in him. It seemed too good to be true.

She supposed she believed him because she wanted to. She had other things to worry about, such as money. She'd finally found a half-decent flat on the edges of Southbury but she needed a deposit. She'd resolved to ask her clients for some money on account at their next meeting on Monday.

Meanwhile she decided to say nothing to Harry until it became definite.

And Jack Doyle? Though he intruded into her thoughts, he did not materialise in person. She assumed he was still abroad until Harry pulled a disappearing act while out walking in the woods. She didn't take long to find him.

Instinct led her to the big house and there he was, in the stable yard, playing makeshift cricket with a plank of old wood and a tennis ball.

He wasn't on his own, of course. Cricket was hardly a one-man sport.

She could have barged in and demanded he come home. Instead she stood at the end of the stable block, her heart heavy as lead as she watched the two together, Jack Doyle calling out advice before bowling the ball, shouting 'good shot' on the occasions Harry hit it.

Another man, smaller and stockier in build, was fielding. She heard his American accent and guessed he might be Jack's partner.

Her eyes switched back to Jack and Harry, laughing at some joke, their heads held at exactly the same angle. How could kinship go unrecognised when she could see it so clearly?

She marvelled at it, even as she wanted to run from any acceptance of it. Ten years she'd spent denying Harry a father in his life, all that time convinced she could be everything to him.

So when had she played cricket with him? Any sport, for that matter? Or even made him laugh so loudly?

Stop it! she told herself, before madness made her do something they'd all regret.

Harry was playing with Jack Doyle because it was Sunday morning and he had nothing better to do. It was a makeshift game of cricket, that was all. Not some mysterious, sacred bonding rite between father and son.

Just imagine if she did go wading in with true confessions. *This is your father, Harry.* She could visualise Harry's shock giving way to hope and expectation. But Jack's reaction? A man who had reached his thirties, avoiding attachments on the way? Somehow she didn't think he'd get beyond shock.

She retraced her steps to the cottage and was sitting at the kitchen table, thinking of everything and nothing, when Harry eventually reappeared.

'Sorry I'm late.' He made an effort to sound contrite but his face was flushed with pleasure.

'That's all right.' She went to the fridge to fetch their salad lunch.

Harry squinted her a look as he sat down to eat. He lasted a couple of minutes before conscience got the better of him.

'I wandered up the road to see if they've finished laying the Tarmac,' he continued carefully.

'And have they?' Esme enquired, though they both knew the road to the West Gate had been complete for more than a week.

'Pretty much,' he confirmed, and finally volunteered, 'Mr Doyle was in the yard. He's back from Japan.'

'Is he?' She managed to keep her voice level.

Harry nodded. 'He was with a friend of his called Sam, who's got a son about my age. We played a little cricket because the boy doesn't know how to play. He's American.'

'I didn't—' Esme caught herself up from saying she hadn't seen any other boy. Presumably he'd been in the house when she'd been spying—no, not that—watching.

'You didn't what, Mum?' Harry waited for her to finish.

'Nothing.' She forced a smile, dismissing its importance.

'You don't mind, do you, Mum?' he asked next.

Esme could have said, *Yes, she did mind.* For all sorts of reasons it hurt. But she couldn't bring herself to be a killjoy.

'No, not really,' she lied.

'Good.' Her son brightened. 'Because Jack says I have to ask you if I want to go back after lunch to see Eliot... That's the American boy.'

She supposed she had to give Jack credit. He was playing by some sort of rules. But did he know how hard it would be for her to refuse?

'You can go if you like,' she said quietly.

'Cool.' Harry awarded her the ultimate accolade and, finishing his chicken salad in record time, was gone before she could even offer dessert.

She could have spent the Sunday afternoon sitting around feeling sorry for herself. It was tempting. Instead she checked over the portfolio she was to present the following afternoon. The Claremonts hadn't been the easiest of clients, often unable to agree between themselves what they wanted, but Esme was quite proud of the work she'd done.

Satisfied, she spent the rest of the time sorting through the tiny spare bedroom next to hers. They used it for storage and over the years everything that had been deemed useful but not currently in use had been thrown in there. Now she had to get ruthless or they would never fit their possessions in a smaller flat.

She'd created a pile of things to be discarded when Harry reappeared. He asked her what she was doing. She claimed spring cleaning but he clearly didn't believe her.

His eyes clouded over. 'Are we still moving?'

She opted for a vague, 'Perhaps,' rather than initiate an argument, and he didn't pursue it.

When they sat down for tea she decided not to quiz him about his afternoon. Knowing he was spending time with Jack Doyle was one thing. Hearing about it was something else.

Unfortunately Harry didn't share her reticence. He'd clearly had a great time up at the hall, spent mainly with Eliot, the American boy, although there was enough Jack this and Jack that to set her teeth on edge.

'He hasn't moved in properly,' Harry relayed, 'because most of the rooms have no furniture or curtains or stuff. He says he's still looking for an interior designer to do it. Sam, Eliot's dad, reckons it would just be easier if he found a wife first, because if he does it up, then goes off and gets married, she's only going to change it all... I suggested you,' Harry finished innocently.

'As a designer, I hope,' she replied drily.

'What else?'

'Never mind.'

She shook her head.

But Harry caught on.

'As his wife, you mean.' He contemplated the idea for a moment or two before giving it his approval. 'Why not? He could fancy you. You're not that old, Mum, and sometimes you look quite pretty. If you were nicer to him—'

'Thank you,' Esme cut into these backhanded compliments, 'but I think I'd prefer to arrange my own love-life, if it's all the same to you.'

Harry pulled a face. 'Just trying to help... He's very rich, you know.'

'Oh, well, that makes all the difference.' She arched her eyebrows. 'I'd better grab him quick before another gold-digger gets in first.'

'Very funny.' Harry pouted. 'He's better than that Charles. Talk about *bo*ring.'

'*Harry!*' she reproved, then wondered aloud, 'You haven't been talking about him to Ja—Mr Doyle, have you?'

A pause followed in which Harry's cheeks reddened, even as he said, 'Why would I do that...? Must go and do my spellings.'

Esme was tempted to call him back and give him a grilling. But what was the point? Even if he gave her a blow-by-blow account of what had been said, she couldn't *un*say it. And was it Jack Doyle's fault if Harry had suddenly developed a talkative streak?

Still, it worried her what else Harry might tell him. Simple stuff, like being ten, not nine. Big stuff like the fact he'd never met his dad, didn't even know his name. What might Jack make of that?

She realised that for peace of mind she would have to forbid Harry to go up to the house.

She waited until his bedtime, creating an opening while she tucked him in. 'Harry, about Mr Doyle—'

'Jack,' he corrected. 'That's what *he* says I should call him, Mum.'

'OK. Jack.' She tried again, 'I know you like him—'

'Yeah, who wouldn't?' Fortunately the question was rhetorical. 'It isn't just his cool car and stuff, Mum. He's really funny. And he's mega-clever—'

'I'm sure.' Esme was in no mood to listen to Jack Doyle's virtues being extolled. 'But perhaps it's best if you don't go up to the main house again.'

'Why?'

Why? Esme didn't have a ready answer.

Harry supplied his own. 'Just because you don't like him.'

'I…I…no.' Esme wished it were that simple. 'It's not a question of that. It's more…a matter of privacy. You have to respect his.'

'But it's all right if he invites me?' Harry came back quick as a flash.

'I…I…yes, I suppose.' She couldn't bring herself to forbid all contact.

Even when Jack himself phoned later, she couldn't quite do it.

He got to the point after a bare exchange of greetings. 'I thought I should check with you. Harry did have your permission to be here?'

'Yes.' She supposed he had. 'But if he's any trouble—'

'No trouble at all,' he reassured her. 'It was great for Eliot—Rebecca and Sam Wiseman's boy—to have another kid around. Tell him to come up whenever he likes.'

Esme groaned inwardly.

'That's good of you,' she hid behind politeness, 'but we will, of course, be moving soon.'

'You've found somewhere?'

Did he really care? 'Possibly.'

'Well, if you need any help moving…'

Was that an offer? Sounded like it. Perhaps he couldn't wait to get rid of her.

'I'll call a removal firm,' she countered rather ungraciously.

It drew a brief laugh in response. 'You do like life difficult, don't you, Esme?'

'Life *is* difficult,' she replied heavily and precluded comment by putting the phone down.

She should have felt satisfied. She wanted him to know she could do without him and his philanthropy. But did she have to be so rude about it?

Yes, she decided, if Jack Thick-Skinned Doyle was to get the message. But she still felt churlish and ungrateful.

She woke on the Monday in not much better a mood but psyched herself up to be positive for her afternoon meeting with her clients.

As things transpired, she could have spared herself the effort. She turned up at the appointed time, only to wait almost an hour for Edward Claremont to appear in his top-of-the-range saloon.

He was unapologetic and showed scant interest in the finished drawings. Esme began to get a bad feeling, but she pressed ahead with a request for the part-payment. It was then that Edward Clarement dropped his bombshell. There would be no refurbishment because he had decided to sell the house. And no, he didn't feel any obligation to pay her for time already spent. She had been hired by his wife and his wife had run off with someone else.

Scarcely Esme's fault, she tried to reason with Edward Claremont and found herself cursorily dismissed without so much as a thank-you.

She drove home in a semi-daze, thinking of all the money she'd just lost and wondering if her luck could get any worse.

It could and did, two miles from home, when her car suddenly coughed and died on her. She realised almost immediately what was wrong. Petrol. She'd meant to refill on the journey home but being sacked had driven all thought of it out of her head.

She had three choices: call the rescue services, hitch a lift, or walk. She consulted her watch and realised none would have her home in time for Harry. Thank God for the mobile phone.

She switched it on and called the school. Surely they could keep him there till she turned up.

Never the friendliest of ladies, the school secretary sounded more sniffy than usual, and insisted on putting the headteacher on the line, who informed her that her *friend* had already collected Harry.

What friend?.

A man they'd presumed to be her boyfriend.

'What was his name?' Esme tried to quell panic.

'I—I'm not exactly sure,' Mrs Leadbetter admitted. 'He didn't really introduce himself.'

'What did he look like?' Esme asked before more time was wasted.

'Well, let's see. Tall, dark-haired.' The headteacher paused before adding, 'Rather good-looking... Your son definitely knew him, Mrs Hamilton, and he came in response to our call.'

'*Your* call?'

'Yes, there was some trouble at school today,' the headteacher revealed, 'and we felt it better that Harry go home early.'

'Trouble?'

'A fight between Harry and another boy.'

'Is Harry hurt?'

'Not badly,' the head stated, 'and your son did initiate the conflict, *Ms* Hamilton. As he refused to take blame or return to his classroom, we had no real choice but to send him home.'

Esme refused, in turn, to believe this story. 'Harry's never been in a fight before. You are aware he's being bullied?'

'Yes, well…' The headteacher was clearly choosing her words. 'We are aware the situation is somewhat more complex than we originally thought. If you could come in tomorrow to discuss the matter…?'

'We'll see.' Esme wanted to talk to Harry before she agreed to anything. 'I have to go,' she added, and rang off.

Then she checked her message service on the mobile and found two. The first was an appeal from the school to telephone them. The other was from Jack Doyle, simple and to the point:

'Harry's school called. Harry's fine but there's been some discipline problem. I'm going to collect him. He'll be at the house. Don't panic.'

Don't panic! She scowled at the handset even as she followed the advice and took a couple of deep breaths before assessing the situation.

Harry was all right. That was the main thing. Any trouble with the school could be sorted. She just had to get home.

She tried the car again, more in hope than expectation, before calling the rescue service. They promised to be there before dark. As it was six hours before nightfall, she decided not to wait.

She started along the verge, planning to walk all the way, but, barely a hundred yards on, a car drew up beside her.

It was an elderly couple. They had seen her abandoned car and were concerned about her walking alone. Would she like a lift?

Accepting a ride from total strangers was not usually the wisest thing to do but this elderly couple couldn't have looked more innocuous, and they were probably right. She would be safer inside their car than wandering along the side of the road.

She climbed into the back and, after a polite exchange of names and destinations, she was driven at a surprisingly brisk pace right to the West Gate. Her good Samaritans waited while she operated her remote—fortunately she'd remembered to slip it into her handbag—before driving off with a wave.

Their kindness helped offset some of the bad things that had happened that day, but by the time she'd walked the length of the drive she was wound-up again.

She had to pick her way through dismantled scaffolding, rubble and various other building-site paraphernalia before she could even reach the back door, wide open to the world.

The kitchen was a hive of activity, with men hammering, plastering, tiling. Otherwise it was empty. No units, sink, cooker. Just a void waiting to be filled. Momentarily distracted, she wondered what would replace the ancient Aga and equally ancient cabinets.

No one challenged her as she continued through to the hall, locating voices coming from the drawing room. She geared herself up, before knocking briefly and entering. The room had a minimum of furniture—chairs, a couple of sofas and some occasional tables—and her eyes went between the two occupants, neither of whom was Harry.

'Where is he?' she demanded without preamble.

'Upstairs in the attic.' Jack rose to his feet, as did his companion. 'He's playing with Sam's son, Eliot.'

'Right.' Esme willed herself to keep calm until she knew the whole story.

'This is Sam,' Jack introduced the other man, 'married to Rebecca, whom you've already met. Sam, this is Esme, Harry's mother.'

'Pleased to meet you.' The American approached with his hand outstretched.

'Hello.' Esme took it briefly.

'Nice boy you have there,' he volunteered with a smile.

'Thank you,' Esme replied, but her tone was stiff.

He took it as his cue to say, 'I think I'll go and see what the guys are doing.'

Jack nodded, approving the move, and waited until his friend had left the room before speaking.

'I can guess you're mad,' he began as the mask of politeness slipped from her face, 'but let's at least sit down and discuss this rationally.'

He indicated a seat and retook his own. Esme perched on the end. She hadn't come for any cosy chat.

'Why should I be mad?' she replied rhetorically. 'My son has been sent home with someone the school's never met before and who has no permission to take him, but what the hell!'

'OK. OK.' He held up his hands. 'Maybe I made the wrong judgement call but what else could I do? They rang you first before trying the second line of contact, your mother.'

'My mother?' What had her mother to do with this?

'Or her old number, at least,' he explained, 'which seems to have been reassigned to me.'

'Oh.' And Esme had failed to update Harry's records. 'You could have told them you had nothing to do with him, couldn't you?' she argued next.

'I could,' he agreed, 'and probably would have, had Harry not told them otherwise.'

'What precisely?' She didn't like the sound of this.

'That I was a good friend of yours—' his lips twisted at the irony '—and we lived in the same place.'

'I see.' Esme wished she didn't. 'But you corrected any wrong impressions, right?'

'I would have,' he claimed, 'only your headteacher was already several conclusions ahead of herself, casting me in the role of honorary stepdad, and it seemed easier to go in person to explain our relationship.'

'We don't have one,' Esme felt the need to remind him.

'Yet,' he qualified, glancing across at her.

Esme chose to ignore it in favour of finding out what had happened next.

'You cleared things up at the school?' she prompted.

'Tried to,' he confirmed.

Esme didn't like the sound of that. 'And?'

'I'd barely set foot in her office when the headteacher

launched into an account of the afternoon's events,' Jack relayed. 'Which, in summary, are: Harry pushes boy over, punches him several times, gets pulled off, marched to head's office, then refuses to account for his actions, leading to his removal pending further investigation.'

'What?' Esme said in disbelief. 'He's been expelled.'

'Suspended, I think is the word the head used.'

'And you just let them do that?'

'As opposed to what?' He tilted his head in enquiry.

'I…' Esme couldn't think of an obvious answer and confined herself to scowling, 'You believe Harry would start a fight?'

'Sufficiently provoked, yes,' Jack countered. 'Any boy would. Which is what I told the headteacher when she finally drew breath.'

So he had defended Harry. She didn't know whether to be pleased or resentful.

'I also told her,' he ran on, 'that before punishing Harry she should ask herself why a normally well-behaved boy had acted so much out of character. And that if she excludes Harry without doing so first, then she may expose herself to litigious action.'

Esme wasn't sure whether to applaud or be horrified. 'What does that mean exactly?'

'We'll sue her,' he translated.

Now Esme was horrified. 'What did she say?'

'What you'd expect.' He gave a slightly vulpine smile. 'Backtracked immediately. Promised to look into the matter. Granted Harry holiday leave in the interim.'

He looked satisfied, as well he might. If Esme were honest, she had often longed but never dared to challenge the officious Mrs Leadbetter.

'You can yell and shout at me now,' Jack offered, 'because I know I overstepped the mark.'

Esme had come prepared to do just that, but now recognised that, despite their ongoing conflict, he had gone to bat for Harry.

'How is Harry?' she asked instead.

'Physically fine,' he relayed, 'apart from a bruise on his shin and a couple of scratch marks on his neck. I'm told the other kid looks a lot worse.'

Typically male response. 'Is that meant to cheer me up?'

'No, but it's certainly made Harry feel better,' he told her evenly. 'It seems said boy and his twin brother have been dogging him for months.'

And *she* hadn't done anything about it. Jack didn't say so, perhaps didn't even think it, but it was true none the less. She had buried her head in the sand, hoping everything would sort itself out.

'I should also warn you,' Jack added, 'that he's adamant about not returning to the school. Apparently it's full of sociopaths and children of limited intellectual capacity.'

'He said that?'

'No, that's just a précis, excluding politically incorrect words like loony and moron.'

Esme shook her head, refusing to accept it was that bad. 'You went there, didn't you?'

He nodded. 'Yeah, and it wasn't much different then. Whoever said school days are the happiest days of your life didn't go to City Road Primary.'

Esme stared at him in surprise. He'd never complained in the past. She'd always been the one to whinge on about how much she hated her boarding-school.

'But you did so well,' she insisted.

'Different era.' He shrugged. 'Nowadays they seem to go for the lowest common factor, leaving a kid like Harry screaming inside with boredom.'

Was he? In the early days she'd asked him about what he did at school but over time she'd become discouraged by answers of 'not much' and 'I can't remember.' But she'd always assumed that it was her questioning that had bored him, not school itself.

'The kid is doing the most basic arithmetic at school,' Jack commented, 'while coding his own computer programs at home.'

'OK, so quantum physics isn't on the curriculum.' Esme was put on the defensive. 'What can I do about it?'

'I'm not attacking you, Esme.'

'Aren't you?'

It felt like it.

'I'm just saying,' he continued patiently, 'that there's a risk he'll become disaffected before he even reaches secondary school.'

'So what's your solution?' She turned on him. 'I assume you have one.'

Jack understood he was stepping on sensitive ground but went ahead anyway. 'Have you considered private school?'

'Of course,' she threw back, 'but I choose to eat instead.'

If he registered the sarcasm, he didn't show it. His expression remained that poor-pathetic-Esme one she was coming to know and detest.

'What about your mother?' he suggested levelly.

'What about my mother?' she repeated, stony-faced.

He was undeterred. 'Couldn't she help?'

Esme parried the question with a shrug. It was more a case of *wouldn't* than couldn't.

'Then I could help,' he added.

'You?' Esme hadn't seen it coming. 'Why should you help?'

Oh, God, had he found out? Had Harry let something slip that had enabled him to put two and two together and come up with four?

To her further confusion, Jack seemed to go off on a tangent, saying, 'Do you remember my going on to Addleston Boys Grammar to do A levels?'

She nodded. 'You went on a scholarship.'

'A part-scholarship. The rest was paid for by your father,' he told her.

Esme's eyes widened at this revelation. 'Why would he have done that?'

He steepled his fingers, considering his next reply. 'He was a generous man.'

Esme couldn't argue with that. Her mother had always

claimed their father's generosity—and gambling—had landed them in the poorhouse.

It could be true, yet she sensed Jack was holding something back. 'Did my mother know?'

He shook his head. 'It was a secret—between him and *my* mother…I don't really think you should tell her now, either.'

Because her mother loathed him? Or for some other quite different reason?

She recalled her father and Mary Doyle, talking in the kitchen at times, laughter between them not uncommon, on much friendlier terms than her mother had ever been with her domestic, as she'd always referred to Mrs Doyle.

'You're saying…'

'I'm saying nothing,' he stated flatly, 'other than the fact your father was good enough to give me a leg up in life. That I repay the debt to his grandson seems only fair.'

He made it sound simple, but surely she couldn't accept such an offer from Jack Doyle? No, perhaps not from him, but from Harry's father? Could that be wrong?

'No strings attached,' he added as she hesitated.

'Strings?'

'As in having to sleep with me in return.'

Esme's mouth went into a line. Did he have to be so blunt?

'If that's meant to be reassuring—'

'It is, yes.'

'—then I wouldn't consider a career in public relations if I were you.'

He laughed briefly. 'You know us computer geeks—not famous for our people skills.'

Esme pulled a face in reply. Whatever Jack Doyle was, he was no one's idea of a geek. Too handsome, for a start, and skilful enough in manipulating people when he chose. He'd seduced her rather effortlessly.

And somehow he seemed to have seduced her son. Normally taciturn, Harry had told him more in one afternoon than he had her in months.

She was jealous. Awful, but true. Man and boy had made

some connection without any knowledge of the real one between them.

And if they ever found out?

She suddenly felt scared. She loved Harry so much, to lose him would be unbearable. But what if he was given the choice—the simple life he led with her versus the things Jack could offer him?

No, it wouldn't come to that.

She pushed up from her chair. 'I'd better get Harry?'

He followed her to his feet 'I'll show you up to the attic.'

'I think I can find the way.'

'Of course.'

He'd forgotten. Sometimes she forgot herself. Another life.

They walked out into the hall and she let him take the lead. It was *his* house, after all. A fact she no longer minded. Harry was now the main issue.

'If you'll consider it, anyway,' Jack resumed as they climbed the staircase, 'my paying for Harry's education.'

She wanted to refuse point-blank, but did she have the right to turn him down on Harry's behalf?

'I will. Thank you.' She forced the words out.

If he'd mocked her half-hearted gratitude, it would only be what she deserved, but it seemed Jack Doyle was a bigger person than her.

'You only have to ask, OK?' he added simply.

She nodded in acknowledgment as they walked along the gallery to the closed stairs that led to the attic.

In her family's day this third storey had been used for junk, and the change was quite remarkable. An office suite now ran the length of the floor, skylights flooding the space with light, and banks of computers and other high-tech equipment built into the walls.

Harry was glued to one screen with a slightly older boy, playing an adventure game.

'Harry.' She tried to draw his attention. *'Harry.'*

Momentarily distracted, he turned to utter a, 'Hi, Mum,' before fixing his eyes back on the monitor.

Esme frowned at his back. She'd expected to find him

contrite or perhaps upset and was somewhat cross that he wasn't either.

'Harry,' she said more firmly, 'we have to go.'

'Five minutes.' This time he didn't even turn.

Esme breathed in deeply. She didn't want to create a scene with Jack Doyle as witness, but said with quiet insistence, 'No, now, Harry. We have to talk about what happened at school.'

She finally gained his attention. Well, enough of it for him to swivel round and announce, 'I'm not going back. I can't, anyway. They expelled me.'

'No, they didn't—' that wasn't Esme's impression '—we just have to go in and see Mrs Leadbetter and clear the whole thing up.'

'I'm not going.' His expression became mutinous and he glanced towards the man standing at her shoulder for support.

But Jack shook his head, a gesture Esme caught out of the side of her eye.

'Harry...' She tried to appeal to reason.

Harry, however, presented his back again. Esme was shocked by his rudeness but too inhibited to react.

Not so Jack. He crossed to a wall switch and abruptly turned off the power.

Even Esme knew that was a bad thing to do to a computer.

Both boys looked up at him, slightly fearful.

'Eliot—' he inclined his head to the door '—go get a drink or something.'

'Sure.' The boy didn't need telling twice.

Neither did her son. 'Harry, your mother's speaking to you.'

She immediately had Harry's full attention, courtesy of Jack Doyle.

'You want me to go?' Jack added to her.

She made a slight face that could have been interpreted as yes or no.

At any rate, he stayed, taking a step back to lean against some shelving.

Harry stared at her resentfully.

'Look, I'm not angry with you,' she stated from the outset, 'I simply want to know what happened.'

'I started a fight.' No hint of regret.

'Was it one of the bullies you hit?' she guessed.

He nodded. 'Dean Jarrett.'

'Why?' she asked simply.

He chewed on his lip, in no hurry to give an answer, and glanced sideways to Jack.

Esme raised a questioning brow at the man, too.

Jack shook his head. 'He hasn't told me.'

'Dean said things,' Harry finally admitted.

'Things?' Esme echoed.

'Bad things.' Harry was clearly reluctant to be specific.

If Esme felt impatience, she quelled it.

'Look, Harry,' came from Jack, 'giving the story in installments isn't going to make it sound any better.'

Esme didn't appreciate this interruption, fearing Harry would clam up altogether.

But she couldn't have been more wrong, as he suddenly began to relay, 'Dean wanted me to give him some of my pocket money, otherwise he and Dwayne were going to bash my head in. I said I'd get my dad to bash his in, but he just laughed and said everyone knows I don't have a dad because…because you're just a posh tart,' he finished in an embarrassed rush.

No wonder he hadn't wanted to tell her.

Esme was speechless for a moment, horrified that children could be so hateful to each other, angry that some stupid parent had gossiped about her in front of their child, but, most of all, hurt for Harry, feeling so vulnerable he'd invented a father.

'Do you know what those words mean?' she asked Harry at length.

'Not really,' he admitted, 'but I know it's something nasty. That's why I hit him.'

'Why didn't you tell the head this?' Jack Doyle asked the next question for her.

Harry lifted his shoulders in a gesture of hopelessness. 'They don't listen.'

'Yes, well—' a determined Esme said '—they'll listen to me.'

But Harry was unconvinced, repeating stubbornly, 'I'm not going back.'

'I'm sorry, Harry,' Esme didn't want a fight with him, 'but you have to go to school. It's the law.'

'Your mother's right,' chimed in Jack.

A beleaguered Esme was, for once, grateful for his support. Unfortunately Harry wasn't. 'I thought you were on my side, but you're not. You're like the rest. None of you understand.'

'We do, Harry,' Esme tried to placate him.

But Harry lashed out at her, too. 'No, you don't or you wouldn't make me go back or make me move house or... or...or marry that stupid Charles,' he shot out as the final straw.

'Harry!' Where had that idea originated? 'I'm...*Harry!'* she called out as the boy suddenly ran past her to the door.

For a moment she was too surprised to follow.

When she tried to, Jack stopped her, a hand on her arm. 'I'd give him a chance to calm down.'

'But what if he runs away?'

'He'd have to scale the gates first.'

He had a point, but Esme was still worried. Defiance was a new thing for Harry. She wasn't sure if she or Harry knew how to handle it. Perhaps a breathing space was needed, but she fretted that he might do something stupid in the meantime.

'I'll go and check on him if you like,' Jack offered, seeming to read her mind.

'Would you?' she echoed uncertainly.

'Yes, of course.' Jack drew her towards a leather sofa. 'Just sit here and rest for a while. You look exhausted.'

Esme felt it and went, unresisting, even as she murmured, 'I can't hang around too long. It's his teatime soon. And there's the car, as well.'

'The car?' He gave her a gently quizzical look that made Esme aware she was rambling slightly.

'It broke down.'

'Where exactly?'

A reasonable question but Esme's mind drew a blank. 'Somewhere on the road back from Dunswich.'

She half expected a derisory remark about these vague directions. She'd forgotten that Jack Doyle could be kind. Had been today, despite her hostility.

'I'm sure we'll find it,' he reassured. 'I'll get someone out to fix it.'

She gave him a sheepish look, before admitting, 'It didn't actually break down. It kind of…well, ran out of petrol.'

'Oh, right.' An involuntary smile, quickly suppressed.

But she'd already seen it. 'Laugh if you want.'

He shook his head. 'It could happen to anyone.'

Esme bet it had never happened to him.

'Anyway, it makes things simpler,' he consoled her. 'If you give me the key, I'll send a couple of the workmen to fetch it home.'

Esme didn't argue. One problem down, more than enough left to go.

'I won't be long,' he promised as she dropped the key in his hand. 'Chances are Harry's joined forces with Eliot in the grounds somewhere.'

He departed before Esme could think to thank him. She *was* grateful. She just found it difficult to express.

In fact, she was beginning to find it all too difficult. The school situation. Her work. Finances. Moving home. Harry… Especially Harry.

Where had she gone wrong? A contented baby had turned into a delightful toddler and from there a young boy, easy to manage because he was eminently reasonable. But, overnight it seemed, things had changed.

Harry was threatening to turn into a rebel before her eyes and she felt powerless to stop it. Worse, she had to face the fact that it was probably her fault.

She had made of him this gentle, well-spoken boy, then

sent him out into a tougher world. She didn't really care that his schoolfriends called her a posh tart—well, of course, it hurt a little—but she cared that he was forced to be ashamed.

And Charles? She'd dated Charles without any reference to Harry and somehow—most likely because of a conversation overheard and misunderstood—her son had come to believe that she was about to foist an unwelcome stepfather onto him.

Then there was the matter of his real father, barely mentioned by her and assumed to be largely unimportant to him. How could he long for what he'd never had?

Only he did. It wasn't a made-up brother he'd threatened the other child with, but a father. It wasn't Jack Doyle's money or computers or big house he admired, but the man himself, as a father figure. The irony of it might have made her laugh if she hadn't felt so much like crying.

And that was exactly what Jack found her doing when he returned. He stood in the doorway, fighting an urge to take her into his arms and offer comfort he doubted would be welcome.

She hadn't let him close since that night at the cottage and then, if Jack was honest, it had been solely for sex. He'd enjoyed it. Of course he had. But it had left a bitter aftertaste, knowing he'd been used. So why did he keep wanting to help her at all? Lord knew, but he did.

Eventually conscious of his silent presence, Esme groped futilely into her bag for a handkerchief before smearing away tears with the back of her hand.

'Esme?' A gentle enquiry.

'I'm all right.' She was furious with herself for showing such weakness. 'Did you find Harry?'

'Yes, he's with Eliot, and already shamedfaced at his outburst,' Jack relayed. 'Sam's taking them for a burger meal, to give you and Harry some time out. I hope that's OK.'

She nodded rather than speak.

Jack came to sit beside her, ignoring the way her body tensed.

'What's wrong, Esme? It's not just the school thing, is it?'

She shook her head. She could hardly tell him of the guilt eating away at her. So she told him something else. The work thing. Countless hours wasted. Her frustration and helplessness. The fact she hadn't seen it coming.

'The bastard!' was Jack's assessment of Edward Claremont when she'd finished her story.

The force of it made tears well in Esme's eyes once more. 'I'm such a mess.'

Jack heard the very real despair in her voice and finally let himself put his arms about her. She resisted for a brief moment before turning her face into his chest and beginning to sob hard.

It was as if a dam had burst. So many tears. He held her and soothed her till they ran dry and she lay quiescent in his arms. He stroked her hair, not trying to touch her in any other way. She was the little girl again, the Esme he'd looked out for all those years ago.

And he was the boy, the Jack Esme had always counted on to make things better for her.

Only it was illusion. Too much had happened for them ever to go back to that time. Life had happened and they had lost their innocence.

Esme felt the heart beneath her fingers begin to beat as erratically as hers and sensed the change. She had to break free, not just of strong male arms, but the longing they created. Had to, even if part of her wished to stay and be loved.

She raised her head and found herself staring into those compelling grey eyes.

'You're not a mess.' A gentle hand curled strands of blond hair behind her ear. 'You're beautiful. Little Esme, all grown up. I can't believe I missed it.'

His voice was a caress, like the fingers now brushing against her cheek. Sweet words, but Esme couldn't bear to listen. He wouldn't be nice to her if he knew the truth.

She shut her eyes against the intensity of his gaze and he cupped her face in his hands. She held her breath, waiting. He put his lips to her temple, a kiss so light she barely felt it.

Then, unable to help himself, Jack inched his mouth towards hers. 'If you don't want this, stop me now.'

Esme heard and understood and shook her head. He might have read it as resistance but for the lips that blindly sought his, and the arms that slid round his neck, and the soft womanly body straining to his.

A kiss, no further, Esme promised herself even as he pulled her back with him on the couch and she groaned aloud at the thrust of his tongue in her mouth. No further, just his hands roaming, searching for skin, pushing upwards inside her blouse. Pulling aside underwear to cup her breasts, fingers rubbing, teasing until she was moaning for him. No further than his body on hers, so plainly aroused, making her long for him to be inside her, loving her hard.

And how it scared her! Wanting him so much. Wanting only him. All her life, only him.

Scared her so much she tore her mouth from his, and, gasping for breath and sanity, started pushing at his shoulders, panicking in case he didn't stop.

No need. The instant Jack realised that the hands which had been caressing him were now rejecting he broke off and let her withdraw to the other end of the sofa, where she desperately rearranged her clothes.

Jack swore softly and, leaning back, ran frustrated hands through his hair.

Esme didn't dare look in his direction. 'I'm sorry. I really am. I shouldn't have let you—'

'No, I should be the one apologising,' he cut across her. 'You're feeling low and I took advantage... All I can say is I didn't plan it. It just happened.'

'I know.' It kept happening to her, too.

'I guess I need to get out more,' he added drily.

Esme recognised it as a joke, intended to lighten the atmosphere, but it didn't make her feel better. If anything, worse. So that was what she was—a fill-in until he met someone else.

Well, it wouldn't be the first time. Visions of Arabella rose before her.

'I have to go,' she announced abruptly. 'Would you send Harry back home?'

'Sure,' he agreed easily.

'Thanks.' Embarrassment made her polite even as she stood and headed for the door.

She was rushing down the stairs before he could respond.

He followed more slowly, reaching the gallery just as she climbed down the second flight of stairs to the hall.

He leaned over the banister and called after her. 'Esme?'

She could have ignored it but felt she owed him. For Harry. And her crying jag. Not to mention what she'd just done to him.

'Yes?' She paused and looked upwards.

He surprised her with a smile. 'I meant it, by the way.'

'Meant what?' she echoed.

'You are beautiful,' he said simply, as if it were fact, not opinion.

And what could you say back to something like that?

Absolutely nothing came to mind.

CHAPTER EIGHT

YOU are beautiful, Esme mouthed in her bathroom mirror, then made a face.

Yeah, a veritable Miss World. Well, after she'd received the crown, cried buckets, had her mascara run and slept in her clothes.

Of course he was just trying to make her feel better.

That was Jack all over. It was coming back to her now, the two sides to him.

She remembered a time when she'd dared to boss him about and he'd called her a stuck-up brat and she'd hated him for days; then he'd come upon her in the woods, distraught because she was about to be sent away to school, and he'd taken her home to the cottage, where his mother had fed her cake and sympathy. She'd been eight to his fourteen.

He must think things hadn't changed much. Poor, pathetic Esme still cried like a baby, still couldn't cope. Well, she'd show him.

How? Go on. How?

What could she ever do that would impress Jack?

She found no answer and, pulling a last face in her dressing-table mirror, she went to wash before Harry's return.

Her car was brought first by one of the labourers and she thanked him warmly. Without her car, she'd be marooned.

Harry arrived later in the evening, brought by Jack. They actually knocked, and when she opened the door Harry stood looking down at his feet. Then Jack touched his shoulder, and he launched into a prepared speech.

'I'm really sorry, Mum,' he mumbled, still not making eye contact. 'I shouldn't have said all those things. I'll go to school tomorrow. And I won't make a fuss if you want to move... And you can marry Mr Fox, if that's what makes you happy,' he finished in a rush.

137

'I... Right.' Esme hadn't a clue how to respond to all this.

But she wasn't required to, as Harry added, 'Is it all right if I go to bed now?'

A first—Harry *asking* to go to bed. She wondered what Jack had done to produce such apparent contrition.

'Yes, certainly.' She echoed his solemnity.

But when he made to pass her, bottom lip trembling, she caught his arm and drew him to her.

She hugged him hard and kissed the top of his blond hair. She felt him sag against her with relief and murmured, 'Love you.'

'You, too.' Harry returned the compliment and the hug but, conscious of watching eyes, she didn't prolong the moment.

Harry directed a, 'Thanks,' at Jack and smiles were exchanged before he finally loped off.

Esme suspected conspiracy. 'Yes, thanks for bringing him back—and the apology-coaching, of course.'

'I gave him a few pointers, that's all.'

'I believe you.'

'You should,' Jack insisted. 'That certainly wasn't any script I'd write him...especially the last item.'

About her and marriage with Charles? She didn't deign to comment.

He squinted at her, assessing her silence, before prompting, 'So, should I expect to hear the banns read this Sunday?'

She pursed her lips. 'Why don't you just ask me straight?'

'OK, then.' He dropped any pretence of humour. 'Are you going to marry this Charles character?'

Esme was tempted to keep him guessing, but what would be the point? The idea of her being in a relationship with someone else hadn't stopped him so far.

'No, I'm not,' she admitted briefly.

His reply was an equally short, 'Good.'

She didn't need his approval. 'Not that it has anything to do with you.'

'Hasn't it?' His eyes caught and held hers, demanding they be honest with each other.

Esme stared right back at him, thinking she could win this

game of truth or dare. But the longer she looked, the more it hurt, and she finally tore her eyes away.

Honest with him? She couldn't even bear to be honest with herself.

Jack realised he'd lost her and switched tactics. 'Because I can't have you swanning off and getting married, once you agree to work on the house.'

'What?'

'Your other commission has evaporated. That was why you couldn't take on Highfield, wasn't it?'

No, that had been the excuse. Did he seriously trust her to do up Highfield?

She felt it only fair to say, 'I've never done anything on that scale.'

'Then the experience will move you up a league,' he reasoned. 'That is how you designers build a reputation, isn't it?'

'Well, yes,' she agreed, 'but you may not like what I do.'

'That's true of any designer I use,' he pointed out. 'But if you don't think you're up to it—'

'I didn't say that.' Esme had some confidence in her ability. 'None of my clients have ever complained.'

'Right, then. Top priority is the reception rooms,' he relayed, as if they'd reached agreement. 'Come up tomorrow and we'll discuss ideas and your fee.'

Esme didn't see how she could afford to turn him down but she still hesitated. 'Look, if you're giving me this work out of charity—'

'Charity?' he gave a dismissive laugh. 'I built a multi-million-dollar business from scratch. Do you think I did that by being a philanthropist?'

Put that way, then, no, and she knew from personal experience he could be ruthless. That was what worried her.

'It's strictly business,' he added.

'You mean that?' She was no longer referring to just the work.

He understood. 'What do you want? A "keep my hands to myself" clause in the contract?'

Esme gave him a baleful look. It was obviously a joke to him. So was she, she suspected. At best, occasional recreation.

'OK,' he ran on, 'how about we say—I won't try to seduce you if you don't try to seduce me?'

'Very funny.' Esme didn't remember *her* ever starting anything.

'Sorry.' Talk about insincere apologies. 'I just don't see what's so terrible about us being attracted to each other.'

'*You* wouldn't,' Esme scowled in reply.

'Me, Jack Doyle?' he enquired. 'Or me, male of the species?'

'Both.' Ridiculous. Why was she even having this conversation? 'I'll work for you but that's all.'

'Fair enough,' he conceded with a shrug. 'Maybe the rest is too much hassle.'

Great. She'd gone from desirable to a hassle within a couple of sentences. Which told her everything.

'See you tomorrow,' he added. 'Afternoon is best for me.'

This stated, he strolled back down her garden path, saluting her a final wave.

Impossible man.

Impossible to work for, too, she imagined, but what choices did she have? She needed the money.

Unless she swallowed her pride in another direction. A temporary loan—that was all it would be.

She tried her mother's number and wasn't surprised to get her answer-machine. Most evenings her mother was out, wining and dining, or socialising at charity events.

Esme hoped her mother knew the old adage 'Charity begins at home,' as she left a message to call her as soon as possible.

No surprise that she didn't that night, and the next morning Esme had to brave school with a reluctant Harry in tow. She went at school start time, and as they walked through the playground someone called, 'You're dead, Hamilton!'

Esme spun round, hoping to spot the culprit, and saw several possible suspects, huddled in a group.

'Mum.' Harry pulled at her arm to move her on.

They were shown into the head's office and Mrs Leadbetter appeared almost immediately. At first, she was polite and conciliatory, but the meeting went downhill fast.

Basically Esme wanted to know what the school intended to do to protect her son from bullies, and listened in disbelief as Mrs Leadbetter talked round the houses before claiming that there was no real bullying at her school.

After that impasse, Esme moved the subject on to Harry's schoolwork. As diplomatically as she could Esme suggested that Harry needed to be stretched, while Mrs Leadbetter cited Harry's lacklustre performance as proof that he was no brighter than average. Again Esme couldn't believe what she was hearing, and asked if the average ten-year-old could do long multiplication in their head. Mrs Leadbetter looked sceptical before pointing out that wasn't part of the curriculum and that they couldn't cater for each individual child's supposed talents. This wasn't some private school with classes of fifteen children and pushy middle-class parents.

Esme lost it then, and, burning her boats with some well-chosen words, sailed out of the school, only pausing long enough to collect Harry from his chair outside.

Once back at the cottage, Harry went upstairs to change out of the uniform they both now loathed, and Esme had calmed down only marginally when her mother returned her call, declaring delightedly that Arabella was home from the States.

It seemed they were having a ball, shopping, lunching and doing mother and daughter things while Arabella reestablished herself on the social scene.

Esme listened with mounting irritation. Her life was virtually falling apart and all her mother could talk about was dresses, the latest restaurant and so-and-so's party.

'Mother,' she finally cut into the monologue, 'can you loan me some money?'

She'd meant to lead up to it gradually, explain her situation, plead even, but it came out as an abrupt demand.

'Well, really, Esme...' her mother was clearly annoyed at being interrupted '...is that any way to ask?'

'No, probably not,' Esme had to concede.

'What's this money for?' Her mother sounded very dubious.

Esme hesitated, loath to admit how broke she was.

'You're not in some kind of trouble, are you?' her mother continued. 'You hear such things these days... Even the minor royals. Injecting cocaine and all sorts.'

'You sniff cocaine, Mother,' Esme stupidly corrected.

Her mother immediately felt she had her suspicions confirmed. 'Since when did you become an expert? Oh, God, you haven't really—'

'Lord, Mother!' Esme finally snapped. 'I'm barely coping as it is, without becoming a drug addict. So, no, I don't need it for my next fix. I need it for shoes for Harry and rent for Jack Doyle, my new landlord, remember? And oh, yes, eating would be nice.'

'Don't exaggerate, Esme!' Her mother's concern had given way to impatience.

It seemed having a drug addiction merited more sympathy than plain, ordinary poverty.

'You have your great-aunt's money and an income from your interior design,' her mother lectured on. 'If you can't manage on that then you'll have to cut back. We've all had to.'

The last remark was almost funny. Even when her father had died and they'd been hit by swingeing death duties her mother had found money for luxuries.

'Forget it, Mother—' Esme already had '—I have to go. Speak to you soon.'

She rang off then, and just sat for a while, reflecting on the conversation. She could have handled it better. No, let's be honest, she thought. She hadn't handled it at all. She'd asked for the money but hadn't wanted it, not from her mother, anyway. She'd sooner take Jack Doyle's dollar in return for services rendered.

This realisation prompted her to get her act in gear and go up to the big house, Harry tagging alongside.

She purposely went round the side terrace to the front door and rang the bell several times before Jack himself appeared.

'I hope you don't mind,' she stated from the outset, 'if Harry hangs around until I can make other arrangements.'

Jack didn't seem too concerned, although he did ask, 'School still giving you a hard time?'

'Something like that.' Esme was reluctant to confess the truth.

Harry had no such reservations. 'Mum went nuclear. You could hear her out in the corridor.'

'Really?' Jack raised an interested brow.

Esme limited herself to a mutter of, 'Impossible woman.'

Harry was more expansive. 'Mum told Mrs Leadbetter that, with such low expectations, she'd be better off as head of the monkey house at the zoo.'

'Harry!' Esme gave him a threatening look, a little too late to silence him.

'I imagine that went down well,' Jack commented, seeing Esme in a new light. 'Remind me never to get on your wrong side.'

Esme could have said he'd never been on her right side but Harry had already proved too efficient an eavesdropper.

'She's a silly old bat,' he supplied now, referring to Mrs Leadbetter.

'Harry!' she reproved again.

'That's what you called her,' Harry reminded her.

'Yes, well, I'm allowed to,' she claimed testily.

She knew she was being irrational before she caught Harry raising his eyes skywards and Jack responding with the twitch of a smile.

'Should I take it you won't be returning?' the man asked of the boy.

'Over Mum's dead body,' Harry quipped, 'and that's a quote… She's going to teach me at home, although I bet I can learn all I need from the internet.'

'I wouldn't exactly agree with that,' Jack rejoined.

Neither would Esme, but no one seemed very interested in her opinion.

'Well, she's not very good at maths, you know,' Harry confided almost conversationally.

One truth too many for Esme, and she cut in, 'Look, if I can interrupt this education debate, do you want us to discuss your interior-design requirements or not?'

It was hardly the way to talk to a client, but then Jack Doyle was hardly like her regular clients.

Man and boy exchanged looks again, before Jack held the door wide. 'Sure, come in. Harry, you can go amuse yourself in the attic, if you like.'

'If that's all right with Mum?' Harry went into model-son mode.

Aware of being humoured, Esme gritted her teeth hard before replying, 'Yes, of course.'

'Great. See you.' He sauntered off upstairs, as if he owned the place.

'Come through.' Jack led the way into the drawing room. 'I haven't really done anything other than get Rebecca to buy a few chairs.'

Esme had noticed them yesterday. 'Do I have to work round these pieces?'

Goodness, she hoped not.

He shook his head. 'We'll donate them to some worthy cause when you've done.'

'Right.' That didn't give her carte blanche exactly, but it was much easier to start from scratch. 'Have you any preferences—colour-wise and overall style?'

'Nothing specific,' he answered. 'I don't like pastels, purples, or anything floral. No frills or fussiness at the windows. I want it in keeping with the age of the house, good, solid furniture, but comfortable, too. I'd prefer to retain the original light fittings and floor if possible.'

'Fine.' Esme scribbled down his comments. 'Tables and suchlike—reproduction or antique?'

'Antique,' he stated, 'if you can find suitable.'

'I should be able to.' She nodded. 'I have a few contacts

in auction houses. You'd want to view anything I bid on first?'

'If possible,' he confirmed, 'although you may have to use your discretion when I'm abroad. I'll give you a credit card.'

Esme was uncertain if she wanted that responsibility, and he read it in her face, adding, 'Look, I wouldn't ask you to do this if I didn't have confidence in you. And let's face it, you have much more idea than I have. You were brought up in a house groaning with antiques.'

Was that another dig? Or just a statement of fact?

'You don't want me to replicate that?' She had loved her childhood home but that was despite its dark formality.

'I don't exactly know what I want,' he admitted, 'but that's the foundation of a successful business. You create something the customer will come to want.'

Esme, not much of a businesswoman, took his word for it. 'Is that what you do?'

'Essentially.'

'What is it exactly you *do* do?'

'Originally I made money from building a search engine for the internet and selling it off to an American software house,' he volunteered. 'Currently I'm setting up a provider, tailored for the global business community.'

Well, she *had* asked. She tried to nod intelligently.

He saw right through it, however. 'I could be talking Greek, couldn't I?'

'More Swahili.' Esme sent herself up. 'I know a few words of Greek.'

He laughed, before assuring her, 'It's not quite as boring as it sounds.'

'I'm sure,' she agreed with mock-solemnity.

'OK, OK,' he replied, 'I promise never to talk computer-speak again.'

'Harry finds it interesting,' she said by way of consolation.

'Yes, I've noticed.' He became serious for a moment. 'He's one very clever kid, as I'm sure you appreciate.'

'Yes,' she confirmed and couldn't resist quipping, 'Amazing, isn't it, with me as his mother?'

'I didn't say that,' he replied quietly, 'didn't even think it. You've always struck me as pretty smart.'

It sounded sincere but Esme still pulled a face. 'That's hardly universal opinion.'

'Your mother has a lot to answer for,' he commented, shaking his head, 'and Arabella, too.'

Just a mention of her sister's name, albeit in passing, and Esme felt it: the usual jealousy.

She couldn't bring herself to tell him that her sister was back in Britain. He'd claimed to be over her, but who knew?

'The offer still stands, by the way.' His voice broke into her musings.

'Offer?'

'To pay for Harry's education.'

He meant it. Plain generosity? Or did he see himself bestowing favours like some lord of the manor?

Did the reason matter? The question was whether she had a right to refuse on Harry's behalf. If Jack Doyle had been some stranger, maybe. But he wasn't.

'Just think about it, all right?' Jack sensed she was wavering but knew not to pressure her further.

Esme nodded, then went back to the subject of colour schemes.

They moved between rooms and she made more notes on his general preferences and definite dislikes. Both would be easy to accommodate and Esme finished this first meeting in a buoyant mood. Provided they could achieve some *modus operandi* that precluded personal remarks and passionate clinches, this was a commission she would relish.

Maybe he felt the same way—that work on his house took precedence over any passing desire he'd had for her. Certainly something between them changed that day, even if it took her a while to realise. A couple of weeks, in fact, before she noticed that they were now talking to each other like civilised adults.

Of course, Sam and Rebecca were around a great deal. Friends as well as involved in his internet business, they had moved into the almost finished ex-stable-block-now-guest-cottage while searching for their own property.

Official school holidays had begun, so she didn't feel obliged to tutor Harry, and most weekdays he spent with Eliot, on the computers or knocking a ball round the newly relaid tennis courts, or being taken up to London by Rebecca to the Science Museum and suchlike, which left Esme free to concentrate on the house.

She had no worries about Harry being in Rebecca's care. Growing acclimatised to the American woman's forthrightness, Esme had found she liked her very much.

The feeling was mutual, and Rebecca often roped her into house viewings rather than a more reluctant Sam.

Esme didn't mind. It was always useful, seeing examples of interior decor. A bit of a giggle, too, as Rebecca and she smiled appreciation at some outlandish piece of taste before collapsing in fits in the car.

If it took time away from her work, Jack raised no objections. In fact, as an employer, he was the most amenable she'd ever had. She said as much to Rebecca one day in the car.

'Oh, everybody loved J.D. in our last company,' claimed Rebecca extravagantly, 'from the copy girl on up. Some people literally cried when he sold it on…especially the women, if you know what I mean.'

'I can imagine.' Esme didn't comment further.

It was Rebecca who went on, 'Not that he was involved with any. I think he makes it a strict rule. No dating employees.'

So that was why he'd switched off his interest like a tap.

'There were others, of course.' Rebecca warmed to her theme. 'He went out with a high-powered lady lawyer for a year or so. Don't quite know what he saw in her… Besides the gorgeous face, great bod and a hundred and sixty IQ, that is.'

Esme laughed as intended. It helped cover up her sudden feeling of inadequacy.

'Hated her, myself,' Rebecca confided. 'So did Sam…

Well, when he wasn't trying to visually measure her endless legs.'

'Jack must have liked her,' reasoned Esme.

'I guess.' Rebecca didn't sound too certain. 'I wonder, though. I have this theory that when guys aren't ready to settle down they subconsciously date women whom they like but only so much. That way, they're in no danger of actually falling in love.'

Laughing, Esme asked, 'You really think men are that complex?'

'No, perhaps not.' Rebecca chuckled in return. 'So what was yours like?'

'Mine?'

'Harry's father?'

'Oh, right.' Esme hesitated to lie to her new friend.

'Look,' Rebecca sensed her reluctance, 'it's cool if you don't want to say. I just thought you might want to talk about it.'

Esme didn't. Well, couldn't. But she didn't want to offend Rebecca, either.

'He was just a boy,' she shrugged. 'An Italian I met on holiday in Rome... You know how it is.'

'You think you're in love,' interpreted Rebecca, 'and it turns out to be lust.'

'Something like that.' Esme supposed that mirrored the truth.

Rebecca glanced across and saw the slightly shamed look on her face. 'Hey, girlfriend, I don't think any less of you. There but for the grace of God and all that... Just don't tell Sam. He thinks I was a virgin.'

Esme's eyes widened at this confidence, and only when Rebecca started laughing did she conclude, 'You're kidding, right?'

'Get you every time, Miss Hamilton.' Rebecca grinned. 'Can you imagine any man expecting to marry a virgin these days? I mean, it's not on. You'd always be wondering if you were missing something, sex-wise.'

By now Esme was used to Rebecca's frankness. Normally she let it pass without comment.

This time, however, Esme found herself saying, 'But what if the first one *is* it, and you don't have to wonder? You *know* you're missing something with the rest?'

It took Rebecca a moment to consider her words. By that time Esme was wishing she'd left them unsaid.

'Are we talking from personal experience here?' Rebecca enquired, sober-voiced for once.

Esme could have gone on. No names, no details. Stick to generalities. But she suddenly lost her nerve.

'No, hypothetically speaking,' she claimed and, looking out of the window, distracted them both with a, 'You have to do a left here, I think... The village is just a mile on.'

'Damn shift,' Rebecca muttered as she slowed to follow Esme's directions while Esme read the exact location of the house they were viewing.

Fortunately Rebecca stayed distracted, and when she did pursue the conversation later Esme was able to feign amnesia.

She was more careful after that. She could allow herself to like Jack's friends but not to forget that was who they were, first and foremost. And Rebecca was about as discreet as a town crier.

A fact Jack obviously knew, when, one day after a discussion on wall hangings and curtains, he remarked, 'You and Rebecca are getting on very well... What exactly has she been saying about me?'

Esme betrayed herself with a blush even as she murmured back, 'What makes you think she's been saying anything?'

'Rebecca's charming and amusing and a good friend,' he declared, 'but she also talks for America.'

'I... She hasn't said much,' she claimed.

Actually Rebecca had told her lots of things. About his life in America. Girlfriends. Cars. Business deals. It was difficult to shut her up and, if she was honest, she hadn't tried very hard.

'I bet.' He gave a cynical smile but he didn't seem particularly annoyed. 'I just hope she hasn't made me out to be Don Juan.'

'Because you are or because you aren't?' She couldn't resist the quip.

'An interesting question.' One he didn't bother answering.

She didn't pursue it, either. She knew dangerous ground when she stepped onto it.

Instead she started to tidy up the swatches and wallpaper-sample books she'd brought for his approval. She was conscious of him standing there, watching her. That was all he did these days, watch. But it could still throw her.

'Anyway, I wondered if you needed some money.' He switched subjects entirely.

'To pay for the curtains?' she queried. 'Can't I use the card?'

'Sure,' he nodded. 'I meant money as in an advance.'

'Oh, right.' He'd already paid her some up front from the sums they'd negotiated.

Well, *he'd* negotiated. The strangest way she'd ever heard of doing business. She'd asked her normal fee. He'd told her she was cheating herself it was so small and he stated the sort of figure she should be looking for. It sounded ridiculously high but she took his advice and amended her quote accordingly. He then knocked her down five per cent, still ending up at almost double her original fee.

Afterwards she'd understood the point. He was teaching her, as he had all those years ago. Trying to prepare her for the big wide world so another Edward Claremont couldn't cheat her.

'It's OK,' she answered now, 'I have some left.'

'That's fine, then,' he responded drily. 'I'll hold on to it, and you can pray my company doesn't go belly up.'

'Why?' Esme looked at him round-eyed. 'Is that likely?'

'Why?' he echoed, gazing back at her. 'Won't you still love me?'

It was a joke. Esme knew that, tartly retorting, 'I don't love you now... And yes, OK, you've made the point.'

'Which is?' he laboured.

'Take the money and run?' she suggested.

'Well, delete the run part,' he responded. 'I have many more rooms to keep you here.'

Another joke, Esme assumed. They hadn't even discussed her doing the rest of the house. But the smile on her lips faded as she caught the way he was looking at her.

'I just don't know if I can keep sticking to the rules,' he added quietly.

'Rules?' Like an idiot, she repeated it, five seconds before her brain caught up.

'Have you forgotten?' He smiled briefly. 'I could jog your memory.'

'I... No.' Esme swallowed hard as his fingers suddenly touched hers.

He took her hand. That was all. It was enough.

Her heart turned over. How could you long for and fear exactly the same thing?

She tried to hide her emotions but he must have seen something in her face. Why else did he raise an arm to caress her cheek?

She breathed the words, 'Please, Jack.'

He knew it was a plea for him to stop, as he moved his hand to her hair, pushing under its blonde weight. 'Why are you so sure I'll hurt you? That's what you think, isn't it?'

Because you've done it before and didn't even realise.

She shut her eyes against the intensity of his gaze. She didn't want him to see down into her soul.

He put his mouth to her ear and whispered, 'I couldn't hurt you, not the way I feel.'

His voice sent a shiver through her, desire threading every word. She felt the same. The trouble was: *she* felt so much more. Finally acknowledged.

'I can't do this,' she groaned back, only they were already doing it.

Mouths seeking, blindly finding, his arms chains around her, hers sliding upwards, fingers burying into his hair, holding his head, his lips to hers, hard and warm. Desire translated swiftly into passion with the clash of teeth and tongues, bruising, tasting, mating. And hearts racing like trains, each breath feeling like the last as their bodies strained to be one.

'J.D., are you…in here?' A different voice, owner talking loudly as she entered the room, fading as she saw.

Sanity returned with Esme tearing her mouth from his. She would have torn free of his arms, too, only he held her fast as he acknowledged the American woman.

'Was there something you wanted, Rebecca?' he asked, totally unfazed.

Rebecca took her cue from him and smiled. 'Yes, but I think it'll keep.'

She started to back towards the door and Esme cried out, 'No, Rebecca, don't go!' before her lifebuoy disappeared.

Receiving mixed messages, Rebecca glanced from one to the other.

With an effort Esme struggled out of his arms and gathered her work together in demented haste.

'It's all right, Es,' Jack reassured, wanting to calm her down.

But she was already heading for the door when her higgledy-piggledy collection of sketches and samples and paint charts began to slide out of her arms. She tried to save the first couple, then gave up and dropped the rest on the floor, abandoning any attempt to restore dignity.

'*Esme!*' Concern, reprimand or just plain surprise from Jack?

Esme didn't hang around to analyse but made for the door and, ignoring Rebecca's startled look, fled for the hills. Or more precisely the sanctuary of her cottage.

Of course she regretted running almost immediately. It was hardly the grown-up thing to do.

So Rebecca had caught them? Big deal. Neither of them was married. They were both old enough. And Rebecca wasn't likely to find it earth-shattering news that yet another silly girl had fallen for Jack Doyle.

Esme backtracked on her thoughts and pressed still on the phrase she'd used. *Fallen for?* Who'd said anything about falling for?

Just because she behaved like a push-over every time he so much as touched her it didn't have to mean anything. It was as Harry's bully had said. She was a *posh tart*. Not the nicest of accolades but how else could she explain her behaviour of late?

You love him.

No, I don't!

Yes, you do.

Rubbish.

Always have, always will.

Just shut up.

'Yes, shut up!' Esme repeated aloud as she caught herself having another conversation in her head.

The doorbell rang. For a moment she considered hiding away, then thought, No, let's get it over with. Tell him what he could do with his job now he'd broken all the rules.

'I'll disappear if you like,' Rebecca offered as Esme opened the door with a rather fierce expression.

But Esme shook her head. The fierce look had been for Jack. Rebecca came almost as a relief.

'I won't feel any less foolish,' Esme countered, and led the way inside.

'Because I saw you and Jack were kissing?' Rebecca said, smiling. 'That's no reason to feel foolish... I don't even know why I was surprised at it.'

'Probably because you think: Now, here's my precious J.D., handsome, smart and mega rich,' Esme suggested with an edge, 'and here's this English girl, average-looking, not so smart, and with a ten-year-old child as baggage.'

'He was your Jack before he was ever mine,' Rebecca pointed out drily, 'and as for your being average, I would die to be as average as you, Esme Hamilton.'

Esme recognised the compliment but nevertheless pulled a face. 'I notice there's no objection to my "not so smart" comment.'

'All right, you're Einstein,' Rebecca said, tongue-in-cheek. 'Whatever, don't run yourself down. Just accept it. The guy's nuts about you.'

Esme didn't know how Rebecca had come to that conclusion but she scotched it with a disbelieving snort.

'Who do you think sent me out here?' Rebecca pursued.

Esme answered with a shrug.

'He thinks he's blown it,' Rebecca continued, 'and you're about to disappear into the sunset.'

'I see.' Esme was sure she did now. 'So he's worried that he's going to have a half-finished house.'

Rebecca gave a loud sigh. 'You really don't know J.D. if you believe that.'

'Don't I?' Esme resented the suggestion. 'You're forgetting. He *was* my Jack Doyle, long before you ever met him, and I learned the hard way just how detached he can be.'

She finished on a bitter note, betraying more, much more than she intended. Old wounds never quite healed.

And Rebecca slowly made the connection. 'He was the first, wasn't he? The one you talked about.'

Esme cursed her new friend's astuteness, then reminded herself whose *old* friend Rebecca was. 'I'm sorry. I'm not following.'

'That day in the car,' Rebecca warmed to her idea, 'we were going to view a house. I was saying that everybody should have experience before settling down and you said—'

'Nothing very important, I imagine,' Esme cut in, 'considering I can't remember it... Now, if you've finished saying your piece—or *his* piece, to be precise—I'll say mine, so take notes... Much as I'd like to sail off into the sunset, I need this job. I need the money and I need the experience. However, if Mr Doyle continues to harass me—'

'Harass?' Rebecca's eyes rounded in disbelief. 'Come on, you don't expect me to say this to him, do you?'

'What would you call it?' Esme demanded testily.

'Well, from where I was standing, honey,' Rebecca drawled back, 'you sure seemed to be enjoying this harassment.'

Esme coloured darkly. Whose side was Rebecca on? His, of course, she reminded herself.

'He is currently my employer,' Esme intoned primly. 'What would you have me do—slap his face?'

'So you just had to grin and bear it?' Rebecca gave a mock-pout. 'Poor little Esme.'

'All right.' Esme conceded the point. 'I wasn't altogether unwilling. He's an attractive man and he knows how to kiss. But that doesn't mean I want to be used as...a sexual diversion any time he feels like it.'

'But if he was actually serious about you?' Rebecca countered immediately.

'He isn't.' Esme wasn't a fool.

'But say he was.' Rebecca wouldn't give it up.

'Then fine,' Esme retorted. 'He can get down on one knee, ask me to marry him, and we'll live happily ever after.'

It was pure sarcasm, picked up by Rebecca although she was deadpan as she enquired, 'Do you want me to relay all that?'

'Do you want me to kill you?' Esme threw back.

Rebecca grinned in response. 'OK, so what do I say? No more hanky-panky or you're out of here?'

'Essentially,' Esme confirmed, 'although if you could find a more subtle way of putting it I'd be grateful.'

'No problem,' Rebecca claimed. 'Subtlety is my middle name.'

'Thanks.' Esme's gratitude was genuine, although she rather doubted how discreet Rebecca was capable of being.

Still, it did the trick. While she half expected Jack to come charging down in person, to call her either a liar or a coward, the rest of the day went quietly.

And the next. In fact, if Jack was about, she didn't see him.

It was Rebecca who collared her, waiting until Harry had disappeared with Eliot, to convey a message.

'J.D. says he's sorry that he behaved with impropriety,' she quoted, 'and he will endeavour to act with restraint from here on in.'

Esme supposed that was reassuring. 'If you could tell him

I accept his apology and will continue in his employment until I've fulfilled my obligation.'

'Right.' Behind her serious nod, Rebecca looked suspiciously close to laughter.

'What's so funny?'

'I feel like a go-between in some Victorian melodrama,' Rebecca tittered. 'Never mind, I will apprise Mr Rochester—sorry—Doyle of your intentions. Though, if you want my opinion—' she drawled on.

'Thanks all the same, but no,' Esme cut in sharply.

Rebecca shook her head, implying it was her loss. 'Funnily enough, neither did J.D. I guess there's some people you just can't help.'

Rebecca shrugged, then smiled again, and Esme finally smiled back, having no quarrel with Rebecca.

In fact, in the weeks that followed Rebecca was to prove a good friend when it came to Harry's schooling.

Knowing Esme had yet to find an alternative state school, it was Rebecca who convinced her to try the prep school her son Eliot was destined to attend and who asked its headmaster to consider a late applicant.

Ingrained notions of modesty would never have allowed Esme to declare her son exceptionally gifted, but Rebecca had no hesitation and, days later, Harry was sitting an entrance test, confirming just how high an IQ he had. When Esme admitted the school fees would be a struggle, an impressed headteacher predicted that next year Harry would be likely to win one of the scholarships on entry to the senior school.

All she had to find were this year's fees, and that problem was solved overnight as Jack released another advance in her fees. No coincidence, she realised, but he made it painless for her to accept the money, sending a cheque in an envelope via Harry.

In fact, they had little face-to-face communication any more. He was either abroad or up in London or closeted in his offices in the attic. Instead she'd send him e-mails—a skill she'd finally picked up from Harry—asking for his approval on whatever, and wait for an e-mail in return.

On the occasions they did meet they were assiduously polite. Just as Rebecca had said: more like characters from a bygone novel than real people. But for Esme it was purely a veneer. She told herself she preferred this cool, remote Jack Doyle even as part of her longed for him to reach out and pull her back into his arms and take the ache inside her away.

Nothing in his manner suggested he felt the same way. While her heart kicked up a beat just at the sight of him, his face was so impassive it could have been carved in stone. So what better proof did she need to know she'd done the right thing by rejecting his transitory interest?

None really, but she got it all the same: a final nail in the coffin.

The dining and drawing rooms were all but finished, when he asked her to come up with some ideas for the bedrooms.

'I'm assuming you want the work?'

'Yes, thank you.'

'I'll await your estimate.'

She nodded and concluded she'd been dismissed. She was halfway to the door when he detained her.

'Before I forget—' he waited till she turned '—your sister called.'

'Sister?' she echoed in surprise.

'Arabella,' he reminded her.

Unnecessary, of course. She had only one sister.

'It seems she's back in England,' he ran on.

'Yes.'

'You never said.'

Why should she have? she almost retorted. But she knew in her heart she'd avoided telling him.

'Anyway,' he resumed at her silence, 'she'd like to come down some time this week.'

'Right.' Her tone was leaden.

He looked puzzled and she wondered what he expected—her to burst into song at the notion of Arabella coming to Highfield as his house guest?

'If accommodation is a problem,' he offered, 'I'll put up Harry while she's here.'

'What?' Esme had suddenly lost the plot.

'The cottage is a little cramped,' he added in comment.

Esme caught up slowly. 'You mean so Arabella can stay in his room.'

'That was the idea, yes.' He gave her another quizzical look.

'Fine.' She nodded, feeling more than a little foolish.

'He can share with Eliot, maybe,' proposed Jack, 'in the guest quarters.'

Esme nodded again, then finally remembered her manners. 'That's kind of you.'

'Not really,' he dismissed, 'I like having Harry around.'

And Harry liked being around him. She wondered if she'd have felt less guilty if the two had hated each other.

'Anyway, I said you'd ring back,' he continued, 'to confirm. Apparently she's lost your number.'

So? Esme pondered to herself. Her mother had it. More like Arabella had engineered things to talk to Jack.

Esme said none of this to Jack, however.

Or to Arabella, for that matter, when her sister rang two days later, launching into an immediate, 'You were meant to call me. Didn't Jack give you my message?'

'Sorry, it completely slipped my mind,' Esme said in reply.

'God, you don't change, do you?' Arabella sighed loudly. 'Still a head like a sieve. Never mind, I'm coming down tomorrow. I trust you'll find me space in that Wendy house of yours.'

Arabella laughed as if it was a joke but Esme found she had a sense-of-humour failure. She often did around Arabella.

'Jack's letting Harry stay at the house,' she revealed flatly.

'Lucky old Harry,' Arabella murmured back. 'Ask him if he wants to swap.'

'You're assuming Jack would want you as his guest.' Esme's tone claimed that was highly unlikely. Forget the fact she'd assumed as much herself.

'Who knows?' Arabella trilled back. 'Remember, Jack and

I were an item once. So what's he like now, our stable-boy-turned-dot.com-millionaire? Still dishy?'

Esme couldn't resist a reply of, 'If you like fat, bald men with glasses.'

'Really? I don't believe it!' said Arabella, but from her groan of disappointment she clearly did.

Esme smiled to herself, not caring that she seemed to be turning into a compulsive liar.

'Well, at least he's rich,' Arabella consoled herself.

'But not stupid,' Esme tried to console herself in return.

It didn't work, however. Jack hadn't been stupid in his younger years but he'd fallen for Arabella all the same.

'Meaning?' Arabella snapped in response.

'Nothing.' Esme reminded herself that Arabella *was* her sister. 'When should I expect you?'

Arabella let the argument drop, too. 'Afternoon, I imagine. I'm going to a party tonight, so I won't surface till late.'

'I'll see you soon, then.'

She couldn't bring herself to say 'look forward to it' and Arabella didn't bother with pleasantries either, abruptly ringing off.

I can't face this, Esme thought as she put the receiver back on its hook.

Yet she was going to have to. Just as she had that summer over ten years ago, when she'd watched her beautiful older sister vamp the boy she'd been crazy about for as long as she remembered. And she could do nothing about it.

Unless it was to hope for some miracle. That Jack would suddenly be too fastidious to go with one sister when lately he'd been trying to talk the other into bed? History said not. Or maybe watching the two of them together would have a kill or cure effect? As opposed to a desire to crumple into a pathetic little ball.

No, her best and brightest hope was that Arabella herself had gone fat or bald, preferably both, in the two years since she'd seen her.

And somehow that didn't seem very likely, now, did it?

CHAPTER NINE

No, ARABELLA hadn't changed, Esme concluded when her sister finally appeared late in the evening, dressed head to foot in designer casual and with two suitcases undoubtedly full of other such outfits.

Well, not quite the same. The hair was lighter—lighter even than Esme's, and she had always been the blonder. And there was something different about the face, though it was hard to pinpoint. But the biggest difference was hard to miss.

Esme found herself staring when Arabella cast off her jacket to reveal an impossibly large bosom in an impossibly tight sleeveless T-shirt. Now, that was new.

'Is there a problem?' Arabella dared her to comment.

Esme gathered from that she was meant to ignore her sister's burgeoning cleavage. Hard one.

'No, everything's fine,' Esme rejoined. 'You just might find it a little cold in the cottage. I don't turn the heating on in the summer.'

'I'll tell you if I do.' Arabella cast her eyes round the living room. 'I don't imagine I'll be staying very long, anyway.'

The accommodation had obviously been found wanting. Esme could have cheered. When she'd seen her sister's two large cases, she'd honestly wondered if she was moving in.

'I'd like a bath,' Arabella announced next. 'You do have one, I suppose.'

'Well, there's the tin one,' Esme couldn't resist saying. 'I could put it in front of the fire.'

Arabella looked absolutely horrified.

'Joke,' Esme felt she should add. 'The bathroom's along the corridor off the hall.'

'Very funny.' Arabella didn't like jokes unless she was making them. 'Really, I would have thought you'd have

160

grown up by now, Midge. You always did have the strangest humour.'

Esme didn't remember that. She didn't remember ever having much to laugh about when Arabella was around. Still, now they were adults surely they could manage an easier, more friendly relationship.

'Anyway, I think I'll just go to bed,' Arabella yawned extravagantly. 'The party didn't end till four.'

'All right.' Esme made an effort. 'I'll help you with your bags.'

'You're a darling.' Arabella's red, pouting mouth stretched into a false smile. 'I'll just go up, shall I?'

Arabella took her assent for granted and went ahead, one small make-up bag in her hand.

Esme was left with the two large cases. Well, she had volunteered. She carried them up without complaint.

She was still making an effort the next morning, bringing Arabella breakfast in bed, only to be offered the briefest thanks before Arabella pulled a face at the coffee and rejected the croissants as too fattening.

She tried again at lunch, preparing a low-calorie salad and calling up to the main house for Harry to join them.

'Doesn't say very much, does he?' was Arabella's verdict when Harry eventually escaped from a monologue on the trials and tribulations of her divorce.

Esme was tempted to make some word-in-edgeways comment but claimed instead, 'He's shy.'

'Not very Latin, then.'

'Sorry?'

'Doesn't take after his father.'

'Oh.' Esme's young-Italian story came back to haunt her once more. 'No, not especially.'

Arabella looked at her curiously. 'Assuming, of course, he *was* Italian and not just some spotty-faced groom you met in your horse-mad days.'

Esme counted to ten to stop herself from saying something. While Arabella's snobbery appalled her, common sense told her to let it pass.

'At least,' Arabella continued, 'your little mistake hasn't put you quite beyond the pale.'

'What?'

'Charles Bell Fox.'

'We're just friends.'

Esme couldn't bring herself to discuss her now defunct relationship with Charles.

'You could do worse,' advised Arabella. 'From memory, he's dull as ditchwater, but he's rich enough. And, as the old adage says, beggars can't be choosers.'

'Me being the beggar?' Esme concluded with an edge.

'Well, not literally,' Arabella countered, 'but you're hardly rolling in it, are you? I mean, look at this place. No wonder Jack wanted out.'

Her sister cast a disparaging eye round the cottage.

Esme rapidly lost any ambition to befriend her sister; it was now going to be a case of getting through her visit without inflicting grievous bodily harm.

'Speaking of whom…' Arabella's expression changed to speculation. 'You don't happen to know if he'll be around today?'

'Jack?'

'Who else?'

Esme shrugged. 'I've no idea.'

'Well, maybe I'll just take a walk up to the house,' Arabella planned aloud. 'See what changes have been made.'

'Shouldn't you wait for an invitation?' Esme suggested a little sharply.

Arabella was unconcerned. 'I'm sure Jack won't mind. We're almost family, after all.'

Esme went goggle-eyed at that, considering Arabella had had their mother evict Jack from his home. She said nothing, however, as Arabella draped a cashmere cardigan over her shoulders before departing.

Esme tried hard to concentrate on her work but images of Jack with Arabella kept intruding. It was an awful thing, jealousy.

Wasted energy in this case, too, as Arabella returned within the hour, having found Jack out but Rebecca in and willing to give her the guided tour.

Esme was a little surprised to hear that her sister had apparently hit it off with Rebecca, but that feeling was secondary to her relief that Arabella hadn't encountered Jack. Silly, really, because she knew a meeting was inevitable. In fact, she suspected that was the whole point of Arabella's visit.

Certainly it wasn't to spend time with Esme, as she pulled another disappearing act in the evening to dine out with some old friends, slept late again the next morning, then, when Harry reported Jack's presence in the house over lunch, decided to go and pay her respects.

She came back triumphant. It was the only word for it. Jack had indeed been there and invited her out to dinner.

'More handsome than ever,' was Arabella's verdict on Jack. 'Of course, I should have known that was your little joke. Fat and bald, indeed... I told him, of course.'

'Thanks.' Esme pulled a face. 'He is my employer, you know.'

'Don't worry,' Arabella dismissed. 'He seemed quite amused.'

'Great.' Esme imagined the two of them laughing together at Esme's peculiar sense of humour.

'Anyway, I'm sure he'll forgive you,' Arabella ran on, 'if I ask him.'

'Don't bother.' Esme would sooner go unforgiven.

But Arabella was no longer listening. She was preening herself as she announced, 'It's quite apparent he's still got a soft spot for me.'

Soft in the head, Esme thought as she wondered if Jack had forgotten his last disastrous outing with Arabella.

'And I certainly wouldn't be averse,' her sister continued, 'should he fancy rekindling some old embers.'

It might have been speculation but Esme was ready to take Jack's interest as fact and it left a bitter taste in her mouth. What had she been these last months? A pale substitute?

'I thought he was too common for you.' She reminded Arabella of how she had once dismissed Jack.

'Did I say that?' Arabella laughed aloud. 'Well, one must move with the times.'

Now Jack was rich. Was that what Arabella meant?

'I think I'll go for a long soak, then start getting ready for tonight,' she continued, stretching languidly before making for the stairs. 'Oh, by the way, Jack says you can tag along if you like. The Wisemans are going and they've arranged a babysitter for the boys and Jack's invited this architect chap for you, I believe.'

'No, thanks.' How dared he pair her off with someone just because Arabella had appeared? 'I'm washing my hair.'

Arabella raised a brow at the excuse even as she looked pleased. 'I can hardly tell him that. I'll say you have a headache.'

Esme shrugged, not caring either way. It was true enough—a dull ache had settled between her eyebrows.

While Arabella disappeared for her bath she sat slumped in a chair, wrestling with jealousy at the thought of Jack taking up with her sister again.

She felt no better when Arabella descended later in an evening dress that left little to the imagination. She managed a brave face right up until Arabella departed for the main house, then it was a test of willpower not to cry.

She was glad she hadn't when Rebecca appeared at the door some ten minutes later, holding a glass in her hand.

Esme blinked as Rebecca thrust it at her, muttered, 'Here,' and followed it with two white tablets. 'You have a headache, right?'

There was no sympathy in her tone, just bossiness.

'I... Yes.' Esme was taken aback.

'Well, wash them down!' Rebecca commanded, briskly stepping inside. 'Then we'll go find you something to wear.'

'Look, Rebecca,' Esme protested weakly, 'I don't really want to go.'

'No? What a surprise!' Rebecca took the glass and tablets back from her and dumped them on the hall table, before grabbing her by the arm. 'Tough, you're going anyway, because I refuse to sit back while your bitch of a sister tries to pinch Jack from under your nose.'

'You think my sister's a bitch?' Esme said, a little shocked.

'Doesn't everyone?' Rebecca threw back, already marching Esme to her room. 'Now, what have you to wear? I suggest casual elegance. A nice contrast to over-exposed glamour, I'd say.'

'I'm sorry, Rebecca.' Esme decided to stand her ground. 'I know you're trying to help but I refuse to go in for some vulgar competition with my sister.'

'Because you don't think you'll win?' Rebecca's frankness was stinging.

Esme found herself compelled to be similarly honest. 'I… Yes, I suppose.'

'Well, I'm backing you,' Rebecca announced, 'so put this and this on, then I'll do your hair and make-up.'

Rebecca gave her little choice as she handed her a sleeveless shift dress in pale mauve silk and waited while she undressed and re-dressed before submitting her to a quick makeover.

She wasn't given a chance to draw breath until they were in Rebecca's car, driving to the restaurant.

'Won't Jack think it odd,' Esme queried, 'my sudden recovery?'

'Who do you think sent me to fetch you?' Rebecca countered. 'He's not a fool. A headache, I ask you. Couldn't you think of a better excuse?'

'If he was that bothered,' Esme muttered, 'why didn't he come down himself?'

'He was going to,' Rebecca told her. 'I stopped him. He was kind of annoyed.'

'Oh.' That didn't sound very promising, Jack in a mood. 'I suppose he's cross because I've mucked up his seating plan.'

Rebecca sighed loudly and shook her head. 'You've no idea, have you?'

Esme agreed she probably didn't, but she wasn't so sure Rebecca did either. She didn't know that Arabella and Jack had a history. Or how Esme had, arguably, messed him about since his return. It occurred to Esme that Jack might want her there to witness his reunion with Arabella—revenge for the night he'd come to her cottage and she'd let him make love of sorts, only to spurn him afterwards.

No, too convoluted, Esme decided, and returned to the odd-person-at-dinner theory.

She didn't repeat it to Rebecca, however, changing subjects instead to ask who was looking after the boys, and, satisfied by the answer, concentrated on giving Rebecca directions to the hotel that housed the restaurant.

'Now, go in there and scintillate,' Rebecca instructed when they reached the dining room.

Scintillate? Esme felt more like escaping, but couldn't with Rebecca's hand firmly at her elbow, moral support as they were shown to the table where their party was already seated.

Jack was the first to spot them, and half got to his feet. Did he look pleased to see them? Or merely amused as he slanted her a smile?

Amused, definitely, as he drawled, 'I take it the aspirin worked.'

'I—I, yes, something like that,' she mumbled.

'A remarkable recovery, in fact,' chimed in Arabella, looking daggers from her place on Jack's left.

'Sit beside me, Esme,' Sam invited, 'and make my wife jealous.'

Esme complied, sitting on Sam's left, and Tom Burton, the architect's, right rather than next to Jack.

'You should be so lucky.' Rebecca laughed at her husband. 'Why would a beautiful girl like Esme fancy a middle-aged married man—other than out of pity, of course?'

Sam grimaced but took no offence. 'Less of the middle-aged, thank you.'

'Esme's already spoken for, anyway.' Arabella bestowed the semblance of a fond smile on her younger sister.

Esme looked what she was, bewildered.

'Haven't you told them about Charles, Midge, darling?' Arabella directed at the table in general, but Jack in particular. 'I know it's not official yet, but my mother couldn't be more delighted. The Bell Foxes are such a good family, land-owners round here for generations... Not that that sort of thing really matters nowadays. Well, not to me, anyway.'

The latter was declared with a smile and some judicious eyelash-batting for Jack's benefit.

Esme couldn't believe Jack would be taken in by Arabella or her lies.

Yet the eyes that briefly met and held hers were cool and distant as his tone. 'I suppose congratulations are in order.'

Esme wanted to reply, *No, they aren't,* but others were chiming in their congratulations, before Arabella swiftly re-claimed attention with an anecdote about her own engage-ment and subsequent marriage.

Rebecca flashed Esme a quizzical look, but all she could do was give a helpless shrug and take the menu being offered by a waiter.

She ordered quickly, conscious that she was holding the party up, then entered into conversation with Tom Burton, who was renovating Highfield.

She tried to block out the sound of her sister's voice but it was hard. On form, Arabella could be very amusing and she heard Jack's deep laugh several times before she made the mistake of glancing up, to see her sister's hand resting on his arm. She curled her own fingers into her palms, raising welts, as she fought a losing battle against the green-eyed monster.

Somehow she survived the meal, withdrawing into herself even as she smiled, robot-like, at remarks made by Sam or Tom or Rebecca. If someone had asked her afterwards what was said or what she'd eaten she would not have been able to recall a single thing.

When finally they moved to the lounge for coffee and af-ter-dinner drinks she made her excuses and escaped to the powder room, Rebecca hard on her heels.

'What are you playing at, Esme?' Rebecca's exasperation was evident. 'I said *scintillate,* not *hibernate.* And who the hell is Charles Double Barrel when he's at home?'

'Someone I was sort of dating.'

'Sort of?'

'I wasn't sleeping with him.' Esme realised that was what Rebecca wanted to know.

'But you're getting married to him?' Rebecca said in disbelief.

'Actually, no,' Esme denied. 'I'm not seeing him any more.'

'You're not?'

'No.'

'Then why didn't you say so?' Rebecca demanded.

She obviously thought Esme a hopeless case. Maybe she was, Esme reflected. 'There didn't seem much point. You can see he's more interested in Arabella.'

'No, what I see,' Rebecca replied heavily, 'is your sister practically throwing herself, not to mention her overblown assets, at Jack. That's not the same thing.'

'You don't understand,' Esme sighed, and went on to give a potted history of Arabella and Jack's previous relationship.

'So.' Rebecca was unimpressed. 'That was then and this is now. Do you honestly think a man like Jack is looking for someone like your sister?'

'I don't know,' Esme admitted.

'Well, I do,' Rebecca insisted, 'so get in there and stop behaving like a mouse.'

It was hardly a flattering description but it had a ring of truth. Enough for Esme to rise to the challenge and rejoin the party in the hotel lounge.

Drinks were being ordered. Rebecca beat her to her chair of choice and this time she ended up sandwiched between Sam and Jack.

Having virtually ignored her throughout the meal, Jack gave Esme a long, hard stare before prompting, 'Drink?'

'Bourbon for me,' Rebecca chirped out.

About to refuse, Esme thought, Why not? A little Dutch courage. 'Gin and tonic.'

He gave their orders to the hovering waiter before addressing Esme again. 'How are you?'

What exactly was he asking?

'Your headache?' he reminded her. 'Still gone?'

Oh, that.

'Yes, thank you,' she murmured politely.

Rebecca was right. She sounded like a quiet, colourless mouse.

He stared at her a moment longer.

She thought desperately for something scintillating to say but was already too late, as Arabella distracted him with some remark.

So she went back into hibernation-mode, and, when her gin arrived, drank it rather quickly. She might not have accepted Sam's offer of another if she hadn't caught Jack's sideways glance.

She tilted her head, daring him to disapprove. He confined himself to a slight tightening of the lips.

Killjoy, she mouthed silently, noting that he was on orange juice. Well, *she* wasn't driving.

By her second drink she had become slightly more talkative, but only as far as Sam and Tom Burton were concerned. She resolutely refused to fight Arabella for Jack's attention.

Jack, on his part, certainly didn't discourage Arabella as she flirted openly with him, and Esme had to give her sister credit. Witty as well as glamorous, she shone in company.

Even Rebecca laughed at her more outrageous comments, before taking exception to Arabella's view that having children rarely improved women's lives.

'I don't agree.' Rebecca spoke up. 'Having Eliot improved my life immeasurably.'

'Perhaps, but most women—' Arabella shook her head and suddenly took notice of Esme '—my little sister for one. It messed up her life, as I'm sure she'll admit.'

Esme, not about to admit anything, shot her sister a look that clearly said *be quiet*.

An awkward moment followed before Tom Burton put in, 'I didn't realise you had children. How many?'

His tone was pleasant enquiry and Esme answered, 'Just the one—Harry.'

It was Jack who added, 'You might have seen him round the house.'

'Yes, of course, the blond boy,' Tom guessed through looking at Esme. 'How old is he?'

Esme was caught. She remembered lying to Jack in the first place but Harry had since had a birthday, and Rebecca certainly knew Harry's real age.

'He's ten, isn't he?' Arabella was determined to involve herself in this new turn of conversation. 'I remember him being born around the time of my twenty-first and that was in the May... Of course, you weren't at the party,' she directed at Esme, before relaying to the rest of the company, 'Poor Midge was sent away to preserve the family honour. Futile, really, since she kept the baby and chose to slum it in some high-rise instead. Our mother was livid.'

Esme stared at her sister, open-mouthed at her indiscretion, then glanced sideways towards Jack. She'd hoped to find him uninterested, or at least sufficiently so not to be doing any calculations in his head.

His eyes suggested otherwise, burning into hers, as he asked point-blank, 'Who was the father?'

Jack! came from Rebecca, shocked at the blunt demand, while a general hush fell round the table.

Arabella was the first to recover, malicious amusement in her voice as she volunteered, 'Some Italian schoolboy, according to Esme, but I have my doubts. What about it, Midge? Fancy revealing all?'

Intended to embarrass Esme, it more than succeeded, but it also made her angry.

'Oh, I think you're revealing enough for both of us.' She let her gaze rest on her sister's plunging neckline.

'Hurrah,' Rebecca murmured *sotto voce* at the double-edged remark.

But Jack wasn't to be deflected, grating out, 'So why the big secret?'

'It isn't,' Esme muttered back.

'Then who is he?' He caught and held her eyes.

At that point Esme was almost certain he knew the answer and didn't seem to care if the rest of the world knew it.

She could have withered under the harshness of his stare. Instead she gained strength. 'Nobody. At least, nobody important. So now, if you and Arabella have finished trying to humiliate me...'

She let the sentence trail off as she picked up her clutch handbag, rose from the table and marched away.

She didn't see Jack move to go after her and Rebecca intercept him, warning him not to do anything he might regret. She didn't run until she reached the hotel lobby and heard her name called, and then her escape was impeded by high heels and the absence of any taxis in the rank outside.

Jack caught her on the bottom step, hand clamping on her arm. 'Where do you think you're going?' he ground out.

'Home, of course,' she snapped and, seeing a cab draw up to let down passengers, shouted, 'Taxi!'

'Forget it.' He pulled her with him round the side of the building and she almost tripped trying to keep up.

'Where do *you* think you're going?' she threw back in the hotel car park.

'My car,' he snapped, already dragging her towards it. 'You're my guest. I'll take you home.'

'I'd sooner walk,' she stated, 'and what about your other guests?'

'Rebecca will take them,' he dismissed, escorting her right to the passenger door. 'Now get in, unless you want me adding to your so-called humiliation by airing our business in public!'

His expression told her it was a threat he meant, and he had her pretty much hemmed in, anyway.

Seething, Esme climbed aboard. He slammed the door and actually used his remote to re-lock the car with her inside.

Esme went from angry to furious, rattling at the handle but only succeeding in setting off an alarm so strident she had to put her hands to her ears.

By the time Jack had rounded to the driver's side, used

the key to shut off the alarm and climbed into his seat, she was too shaken to react.

He said nothing until he'd reversed out of the space and then it was a dark mutter of, 'Do you actually imagine I'd let you run away from the truth now?'

It was a rhetorical question Esme didn't bother answering. She expected him to follow it up with a real question but he drove in grim-faced silence and at breakneck speed to Highfield, entering by the West Gate to pull up outside her cottage.

For a moment Esme hoped he would just deposit her there and go, but when she went to open the door he shot out an arm to stop her.

'He's mine, isn't he?' he demanded.

'Do you really want to know?' she threw back.

Esme meant it. She gave him the choice. He could remain ignorant and walk away.

'Of course I want to know,' he grated back.

Esme took a deep breath, then admitted, 'Harry is your son, yes.'

It was what he'd suspected yet he still looked deeply shocked. He released her arm and turned away to grip the steering wheel until his knuckles showed white.

Esme half expected him to challenge it. After all, she'd claimed to have been with other boys at the same time.

But, no, there was just a long silence, followed by a ragged mutter of, 'Damn.'

Hardly a reaction of joy, and Esme took it as her cue to leave and quickly opened the passenger door.

She bailed out, rushed up the path, fumbling for her key, had it in the lock and was almost inside when he loomed over her.

'No, you don't!' He put his foot in the door. 'You think you can tell me something like that and just walk away?'

'What else is there to say?' She rounded on him.

'Plenty,' he bit back, and, pushing her before him, slammed shut the door.

Alarmed by his temper, Esme backed her way into the living room, putting space between them.

'Don't look at me like that!' he rasped. 'I'm not going to hurt you.'

Physically, he meant. He'd certainly hurt her in other ways.

'I just want to know,' he continued harshly, 'why the hell didn't you tell me?'

Esme deliberately misunderstood as she responded, 'In front of your guests?'

His mouth went into an even tighter line. 'When you were pregnant, I meant.'

Esme felt her own temper rise. 'And I would have done that how? Catch a plane to America and go searching for you?'

'I sent you a letter at the time,' he claimed, 'asking you to write back if you had any problems. OK, so I wasn't explicit, but what kind of problems did you think I meant?'

'I received no letter!' she insisted, although she'd begun to believe in its existence. 'I was back in school by then, anyway.'

'Your mother.' His brows drew together. 'She must have intercepted it.'

But Esme was certain her mother had never connected her pregnancy with Jack. 'Why should she do that? She didn't know about us.'

'Perhaps she thought I was after another of her precious daughters.'

'That's possible.'

'And if you had received it? Would you have written back? Told me about the baby?'

'I'm not sure,' Esme answered honestly. 'It was a while before I realised myself, then my mother made arrangements to have the baby adopted.'

'Yet you didn't,' he concluded, and, as some of his fury abated he turned away from her, crossing to a window to stare out on the woods beyond while he struggled to come to terms with it all. 'It's hard to take in. Harry being mine... ours.'

He's mine, only mine, Esme would have claimed a few short months ago, but somehow she'd lost her conviction. She wondered if he was pleased or horrified to have gained a son and where they might go from here.

'Why didn't you tell me when I came back?' he pursued, still facing away from her. 'All this time and you've said nothing.'

'I didn't know how you'd react,' she replied. 'It's not as if you ever wanted to be a father.'

He turned at that, his brow darkening. 'How would you know what I want? Have you ever asked me?'

Somehow Esme had strayed onto dangerous ground. 'I don't understand why you're angry. I was trying to do the best thing for Harry.'

'Like hell you were!' he threw back at her. 'If that was the case you'd have accepted my offer to pay his school fees. You could have taken the money, aware I was only doing what a father would, and still kept your damn secret.'

'I let him come and visit you,' she said in her defence.

'And I'm meant to be grateful for that?' he scorned in return. 'You were going to move away, remember, just so I couldn't be around him, my own son.'

'It wasn't that!'

'Then what?'

Esme shook her head rather than explain the turmoil of her feelings for him.

'God, you Hamilton girls are a class act,' he muttered at length.

Now that was something Esme could rail against. 'Don't compare me with Arabella! I wasn't the one who messed you around, broke your heart in the first place!'

'Broke my what?' He stared at her with little short of amazement. 'You really believe that?'

'All right, hurt your pride if you like,' she amended bitterly.

'That's closer to the mark,' he agreed, 'although perhaps it's time you heard the whole truth.'

'I'm not sure I want to.' Esme already felt jealous enough of Arabella. 'In fact, I think you should leave.'

She managed to sound imperious as she stalked towards the hall. He followed and she actually imagined he was prepared to go. The moment she opened the door, however, he slapped it shut with his palm and somehow backed her into a corner.

'Well, you're going to hear it anyway,' he barked at her. 'I didn't sleep with your sister that summer, although God knows I had ample opportunity.'

'I'm not listening to this.' She tried to shout him down.

He continued relentlessly. 'Oh, I didn't imagine she was really interested in me. She was just bored and I was around. Hell, I might even have been tempted if she hadn't already slept with half the neighbourhood. But I wasn't and didn't,' he finished abruptly.

Esme wanted to believe him but it seemed so unlikely, any man turning down her beautiful sister.

'God, you must take me for a fool!' she snapped back. 'Arabella could have had anyone she chose.'

'That's pretty much what Arabella thought, too—' his laugh was harsh '—which is probably why refusal offended. Hence her complaint to your mother and my subsequent eviction.'

'You're saying—' Esme was incredulous '—that my mother chucked you out because you wouldn't sleep with my sister?'

'Not quite!' He gave a dismissive laugh. 'Your mother isn't that perverse. I assume she heard the version where I was pressuring Arabella to sleep with me... She obviously had no idea what your sister was like, but you did—you even tried to warn me,' he reminded her.

Esme nodded slowly. 'You thought it was funny.'

'It was,' he countered, 'considering I was having to beat her off with a stick.'

Could that really have been the case?

'Why is it so hard for you to believe?' he appealed. 'There

was only one Hamilton sister who caught my eye and it wasn't Arabella.'

'Don't!' Esme couldn't take any more history rewrites. 'We both know I just happened along.'

'God, Esme.' He ran a hand through his hair in exasperation. 'Why do you think so little of yourself? I always liked you, more than liked you. That night we made love it felt so right, even though it was so very wrong, with you just a kid and me so many years older. You weren't experienced either, were you?'

Esme stared at him with surprised eyes, then shook her head. 'No, I wasn't.'

'I guess I knew deep down,' he admitted with a grimace, 'but it helped square things with my conscience, the idea you'd already slept around. If it's any consolation, I've always been ashamed of the way I treated you that night.'

'It isn't.' He could keep his damn regrets as far as Esme was concerned.

'All right, I can't change the past,' he conceded, 'but do you at least believe me about Arabella?'

Esme remained resolutely silent. Wanting to believe didn't make it true.

'You just can't credit that I preferred you, can you?' He made a frustrated sound. 'OK, I'll show you. Where's your bedroom?'

'My what?'

'Your bedroom... The downstairs one, isn't it?'

He nodded towards the short corridor off the hall.

'I... Wh-what are you doing?' she demanded, although he was already doing it, backing her towards the bedroom.

'What I said.' He pushed the door open and her inside. 'Since you won't listen, I'll show you how much I care for you... Light on or off?'

'I—I... Y-you...' Esme found herself stammering.

'Off initially, I think,' he decided, then, in the darkness, leaned towards her to place a hard kiss on her mouth.

'We can't do this.' A rather weak protest from Esme.

'Why?' The next kiss was by her ear.

'Because…because…' She tried hard to focus her thoughts as he pulled the clips from her hair and let it tumble down. 'Arabella. She'll be home soon.'

'So?' He cupped her face in his hands.

'*I* can't do this.' A plea this time.

'Yes, you can.' His lips moved over hers until she began to respond. 'See, it's easy.'

She tried to resurrect his anger. 'Don't you hate me for Harry?'

'Hate you?' He was quietly incredulous. 'You've given me this wonderful son.'

Esme found her own resentment fading. Without it, she was anchorless, swaying in the breeze.

When he said in a soft, persuasive murmur, 'Why don't we make another one?' she was already lost.

He drew her towards the bed. She went, unresisting. He sat her down on the edge. She waited, trembling.

Jack took off his jacket and threw it on a chair, then unbuttoned his shirt to the waist. His hands were unsteady. He had imagined this scene many times over the last months, imagined lying with her naked. He had never wanted anyone the way he wanted her. Yet it was more than just sex, much more.

He sat beside her to feel for her hand and she started like a cat. He wondered if once again she would take off on him. He needed to see her face. He reached in the gloom for a bedside lamp and switched it on.

He lightly gripped her chin and turned her face to his. In the muted light it was all eyes and shadowed cheekbones. How beautiful she was—always would be.

Nervous, Esme licked dry lips. He followed the movement with his eyes, then with one long finger. It was like a kiss, the finger slipping briefly inside, before tracing the outline of her mouth. Moist and ready for the possession of his.

Tender at first, a mere whisper of breath, as he bent his head. Lips warm and hard. Hers parting, letting him taste her, tasting in return.

Breath coming faster. Hand lifting hers. Laying it between

shirt and skin. Fingers on body hair, already damp. Gliding over muscle from shoulder to waist, helping to take off his shirt till he was naked to the waist.

Then his hands were around her, pulling her body to his, all the time kissing her, stealing breath and reason so she barely noticed the zip being slid downwards, was lost long before he pushed her gently back against the bed and drew down her dress to the camisole beneath.

She couldn't have stopped if she'd tried. And she didn't try. She wanted the fingers touching through silk, sliding down straps, spilling her breasts. She wanted the hands cupping her nakedness, a thumb stroking, stroking until the nipple stood erect. Wanted the mouth suddenly leaving hers to cover the hard, swollen tip, drawing whimpering sounds from her as he sucked hungrily at her flesh.

She held his head to her breast while he pushed down the dress further so his hand could move over her belly and slip between silk and skin, one long finger reaching inside. Suddenly there, sliding, slow and steady and strong, giving her pleasure, warm and wet, such pleasure, making her gasp, her legs fall slack with invitation.

Jack felt his own control slipping and dragged at her clothes, wanting her naked, eyes roaming her body as he quickly undressed himself.

Esme's breath shallowed and her heart quickened at the sight of him, honed with muscle and hard with desire. He lay down beside her once more, mouth on mouth, skin to skin, his flesh urgent against hers until finally he pushed his length inside her.

Esme flinched, he filled her so completely. He drew back slowly and she was poised for the next thrust. Deeper than the last. She moaned aloud and wrapped her legs round him. She wanted this, craved each time he raised his body and drove inside her, relentless until she arched and spasmed round him and they came together, crying out the other's name.

Afterwards they lay in each other's arms, bodies slick with sweat, hearts pounding, catching breath. No words spoken, no words needed as he began to kiss her, and touch her, and unbelievably, make her want him all over again.

Only this time he had her straddle him so he could watch her expression as he caressed her breasts before easing himself inside her and showing her a sensual kind of loving.

Complete and replete, Esme wondered how she would ever learn to live without him again.

CHAPTER TEN

INHIBITION had long departed when they heard the sound of the doorbell ringing. Jack was unconcerned, merely murmuring, 'Ignore it,' as he held her to his chest and stroked her hair.

But Esme couldn't. Not when the ring was followed by an impatient knocking on the door. She realised it must be Arabella and she could hardly leave her on the doorstep.

'I can't,' she insisted, and he released her with reluctance.

He watched her as she walked naked to the door and she felt a conflict of shyness and excitement before she shrugged into the dressing gown that hung on a hook.

'You'll stay here?' Esme was desperate to keep him a secret from her sister.

She took his smile for agreement—silly of her, really—before slipping outside and closing the door firmly behind her.

By this time her name was being called by an irritated Arabella. 'Open up, Esme. I know you're in there.'

She was hammering on the door as Esme unlocked it and didn't wait for an invitation before brushing past her.

'Typical!' She took in Esme's night-time apparel. 'You always did hide out in your bed if anything upset you... I assume Jack's gone?'

'Yes,' Esme lied, 'yes, of course.'

Arabella accepted it without question, even as she reflected, 'I wonder why he's left his car.'

Oh, God, she'd forgotten that. Think quickly.

'It wouldn't start,' Esme garbled out. 'I mean, after he stopped it...to drop me off.'

'I suppose he just dumped you and fled,' Arabella continued, marching forth into the living room, 'while I got stuck with that Rebecca woman. She insisted we hang around that dreary hotel for another hour, then got lost on the way home. Incredible. American women can be so stupid!'

Not as stupid as some British women, Esme decided, if Arabella couldn't work out Rebecca had been giving Jack and her time. She blushed to recall how they'd spent it.

Arabella noted the colour and remarked, 'As for you, you may well look ashamed. Talk about amateur dramatics... Perhaps I should go up to the main house and apologise for your behaviour.'

Esme almost laughed at that, but confined herself to a dry, 'Yes, why don't you?'

Arabella frowned, confused by her attitude, but looked ready to take flight before the sound of a door opening distracted them both.

The sisters' heads turned in unison to see Jack make an entrance. Fully dressed, but his unbuttoned shirt was a give-away, as well as Esme's current state of *un*dress.

'Well! Well!' Arabella's tone was strident. 'So we weren't hiding away in our bedroom alone.'

'We weren't hiding away at all,' was drawled back by a totally non-fazed Jack. 'We were making love.'

Esme blushed at such frankness and even Arabella looked taken aback.

The latter staged a quick recovery, however, responding, 'Isn't that a rather grand way to describe a sympathy hump?' before rounding on her sister. 'What did you do? Put on your poor-little-Esme, let's-all-feel-sorry-for-her act? You don't imagine he's serious about *you*, do you?'

Esme had no idea how Jack really felt, but her sister's jealousy was patent even before Jack came to her side and put a supportive arm round her. 'Actually, I'm crazy about her, always have been in a way.'

He gave Esme a look of such fondness she almost believed him. Almost, but not quite.

Arabella was doubtful, too. 'You never looked at her twice when we were young.'

'Didn't I?' He raised a questioning brow to Esme and, at her nod, ran on, 'So how do you account for Harry?'

'Harry?'

'My son.'

It was clear from Arabella's expression that she had never suspected the truth, not even tonight when Esme had fled the hotel. She looked at her younger sister in amazement.

Emboldened by Jack's attitude, Esme confirmed, 'Harry is Jack's.'

'God, that's rich!' Arabella's surprise gave way to recrimination, directed at Jack. 'All that summer, pretending you were too high-minded for casual sex, and you were screwing my little sister.'

Esme cringed from her sister's crudity, although it confirmed Jack's claim that he'd never had sex with Arabella.

'You had your revenge.' He looked at her sister with such contempt Esme wondered why she'd ever imagined Jack liked, far less loved, Arabella. 'Pity you can't have me kicked off the estate this time,' he added with more indifference than anger.

Nevertheless Arabella took it as a threat. 'I suppose you're going to return the compliment.'

'It's tempting,' he admitted, 'but, for the sake of future relations as in-laws, I'd prefer a truce.'

'In-laws?' Arabella picked up. 'You're not going to marry her. I don't believe it!'

Neither did Esme, considering he hadn't even asked her. Just words, she assumed, to put Arabella's nose out of joint.

'He's joking,' Esme told her, and, growing weary of the whole discussion, added, 'I'm tired so if you'll excuse me.'

For the second time that night she escaped, before Arabella became more spiteful and tempted Jack into other rash statements.

She trailed back through to her bedroom and shut the door on the sound of their voices. She stared at her unmade bed and the clothes cast aside on the floor, a visible reminder of what she and Jack had been doing before Arabella had interrupted them.

She could have regretted it but didn't. He'd made her feel so alive. As if she'd been sleeping half her life and he'd been the prince to wake her. Now a total certainty—Jack Doyle was the one and only for her. No comfort in knowing, though, as she couldn't imagine he felt the same way, whatever he'd claimed to Arabella.

When he entered the room again she was sitting huddled in a chair.

'Your sister's gone to bed,' he informed her.

'Good.'

'Have you an overnight bag?'

'Yes, why?'

He followed her gaze to the top of the wardrobe and reached up for the small holdall.

He opened it up on the bed, announcing, 'I think you should move up to the house.'

Temporarily? Permanently? As what?

All these questions flitted across Esme's face before he added, 'Arabella has a pretty undermining effect on you and I don't want her dripping poison in your ear when she leaves in the morning.'

Temporary, then.

'I don't know.' Esme *was* tempted, being reluctant to endure another pointless scene with Arabella.

'Well, I'll pack while you're thinking about it.' He found underwear in drawers, and rifled her wardrobe for several outfits.

More than one night, then.

'I wouldn't like Harry to find me up at the house and get the wrong idea.' She finally voiced her real objections.

He straightened from zipping up her bag. 'And which wrong idea would that be?'

He slanted his head at an angle, waiting for her response. She shrugged. She wasn't sure she had the right idea herself. He sounded more amused by the whole affair than anything else.

'Want me to stand out in the hall while you dress?' he added.

Definitely amused, this offer to preserve her modesty, considering the intimacies they had already shared.

'No.' She pulled a face at him, putting on fresh knickers and jeans under her dressing-gown before discarding it to drag a sweatshirt over her head.

'The woman of my dreams,' he commented drily. 'One who can dress in one minute flat.'

He was smiling so she forced a smile back. She didn't want him to know how it hurt—to wish she really was the woman of his dreams and not the girl next door he occasionally noticed.

What had Arabella called her? His sympathy hump. Ignoring the crudity, was it really like that?

'Come on.' Jack saw all the doubts flitting across her face and wanted her out of the cottage before she changed her mind.

They collected a jacket from the hall and he carried her bag in one hand and guided her up the darkened path with his other. Bypassing his car, they went on foot to the house.

Lights in the converted stables told them that Rebecca and Sam were still awake, but the boys' room was in darkness.

She chewed at her lip. 'About Harry—'

'We'll talk inside,' he insisted, taking out a set of keys to unlock the back entrance.

She thought he meant over tea or a drink, but he ushered her through the side hall and up the stairs. She felt his hand at her back, the pressure light but enough to keep her moving. She wondered if he knew how close she was to bolting.

They passed his bedroom and a couple of others before they reached her old room, still furnished as she'd left it. 'I thought you'd prefer this one, make you feel more at home.'

'Oh, right.' She had assumed…too much, it seemed.

He placed her bag on the bed. 'Give Harry the chance to get used to things.'

'Things?'

'You and me.'

He turned to face her and she awarded him a quizzical look. Exactly what had he in mind?

'Our marrying,' he clarified.

She stared, half laughed, then went back to staring while his face remained deadly serious.

'If you agree, of course,' he finally thought to add.

No, she had assumed too little, Esme concluded, her heart clamouring to shout yes while her head strived for sanity.

'That's a proposal?' She wanted to make absolutely sure.

He nodded. 'I can't produce a ring, but if you want me down on one knee I could oblige.'

'No, thanks,' she returned smartly, willing to dispense with such a tradition. The situation seemed surreal as it was.

'Is that no thanks to down on one knee,' he enquired, 'or no thanks to marriage?'

The former, but Esme let it cover both. 'And they said chivalry was dead.'

'What?'

'That's why you want to marry me, isn't it? To make an honest woman out of me and give Harry your name?'

Jack laughed. He couldn't help it. Such an absurd idea.

Then he drew her to him and placed a gentle kiss on her lips before saying, 'Could it just be that I adore you? That I want to fall asleep every night with you in my arms?' His eyes held hers, telling her he meant every word. 'As for Harry, he doesn't need anything from me to make him a great kid... It's you I want to give my name, Es, you I want to have and to hold. You must know that.'

Not till that moment, and she could only smile back in inane wonder, 'Esme Doyle.'

'You mean...?' He looked expectant.

She nodded.

'You'll marry me?'

She nodded more vigorously.

Jack still insisted, 'Then say the words.'

But Esme chose something more important to say. 'I love you. I love you so much it really does hurt. Is that what you wanted to hear?' she asked, knowing it was from the smile stretching across his handsome face.

'For months,' he confirmed, then groaned drily. 'Only you seemed to prefer putting me through hell.'

'I was just scared,' she admitted. 'I thought…well, it doesn't matter any more.'

'I never meant to cause you pain,' Jack showed he understood, 'and, if it takes a lifetime, I'll make it up to you, Esme.'

A promise so tenderly given it healed any hurt left inside Esme.

In return, she gave her heart, a delicate thing that would beat so much stronger in his care, and said simply, 'Just love me. Love me for ever.'

'And a day,' he vowed softly, taking her hand.

The world's bestselling romance series.

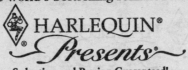

HARLEQUIN®
Presents~

Seduction and Passion Guaranteed!

They're the men who have everything—except a bride...

Wealth, power, charm—what else could a heart-stoppingly
handsome tycoon need? In the GREEK TYCOONS miniseries
you have already been introduced to some gorgeous Greek
multimillionaires who are in need of wives.

Now it's the turn of favorite Presents author

Helen Brooks,

with her attention-grabbing romance

THE GREEK TYCOON'S BRIDE

Harlequin Presents #2255
Available in June

This tycoon has met his match, and he's decided he *has* to
have her...*whatever* that takes!

Pick up a Harlequin Presents® novel and you will
enter a world of spine-tingling passion and
provocative, tantalizing romance!

Available wherever Harlequin books are sold.

HARLEQUIN®
Makes any time special ®

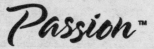